THE HAND...AGAINST THE KNIFE!

The next warrior screamed and charged Ki. The samurai tried another sweep-kick, but the frozen ground betrayed him and he fell hard. The warrior was on top of him in an instant. The Indian was lightning fast, and his knife slashed downward. Ki threw himself sideways and the blade cut through his costume and the muscle of his shoulder. Ki grunted in pain. Then he drove his stiffened fingers upward into the Indian's throat. The warrior choked. He tried to slash Ki's face, but the samurai hit him again and the warrior collapsed, gagging and holding his damaged throat.

"Eeeeii!" a third Crow screamed, bounding across the ring before the samurai could even stand up and meet the charge . . .

WESLEY ELLIS

LONE STAR

AND THE
CHEYENNE TRACKDOWN

JOVE BOOKS, NEW YORK

LONE STAR AND THE CHEYENNE TRACKDOWN

A Jove book/published by arrangement with
the author

PRINTING HISTORY
Jove edition/March 1988

ISBN: 0-515-09492-7

Jove books are published by The Berkley Publishing Group,
200 Madison Avenue, New York, New York 10016.
The name "JOVE" and the "J" logo
are trademarks belonging to Jove Publications, Inc.

PRINTED IN THE UNITED STATES OF AMERICA

10   9   8   7   6   5   4   3   2   1

★

Chapter 1

Jessica Starbuck shifted uncomfortably on the leather cushion of the swaying Concord stage and felt perspiration river down her spine. Beside her, the samurai warrior sat as stiff and silent as he had most of the way across New Mexico. The sun beat down with a scorching fire upon the land of West Texas. Heat waves shimmered across the lonely horizon and hazy blue hills squatted far to the north.

The heat and the dust were punishing inside the stagecoach. Jessie vowed that never again would she take the stagecoach from Santa Fe during the worst of summer. Next time, she would either ride a horse or else take a few men and wagons up from Texas in order to turn the trip into a shopping session. Old Santa Fe was still a major freight distribution center for the Southwest and supplies could be bought at excellent prices.

Jessie sighed and wished that she and Ki did not have another two hundred miles to go before arriving back at her ranch. Her sea-green eyes studied the hard land. She knew that, in country this dry, it would take perhaps fifty acres to carry a single longhorn cow and calf. Not that the Circle Star was exactly the kind of lush grassland that you'd find in Wyoming or Montana. Still, it was a heck of a lot better cattle country than this. At least there was good green buffalo grass for her herds.

Jessie could feel the man across from her watching her again. Jessie kept her eyes averted from his and continued to stare out at the passing countryside. She was accustomed to the stares of young men. With her green eyes, burnished copper hair, and hourglass figure, she had been sought after by men from around the world. Yet she had remained single, dedicated to the Starbuck empire which her father, Alex Starbuck, had bequeathed to her.

Jessie's eyes softened a little remembering Alex. He had been a self-made man, one who had started out with practically nothing but his own dreams and wild enthusiasms. With daring and almost superhuman energy, he had worked day and night for years to take a small San Francisco import business and turn it into one of the richest and most powerful empires in the world. He had done that by refurbishing a small, battered sailing ship and using it to carry merchandise from Japan and China to the United States. He'd soon added a second and then a third vessel and, within five years, had built a fleet of merchant freighters that competed with anyone in the world for the rich oriental trade.

When other men were so backward as to believe that iron-hulled ships would sink because of their weight, it had been Alex who had seized the revolutionary new concept and had his fleet refitted so that it could withstand the rigors of the trade. He had then built his own steel mill and iron mines to refine the ore. When the transcontinental and other railroads had begun to lay track across the great continents of the world, it had been Starbuck steel mills that had rolled thousands of miles of track out of their molten buckets. Firmly convinced that the railroads would emerge as the major

2

powers of the West, Alex had purchased their stock in volume. As wealth built upon wealth, pyramiding into a fortune that few even guessed, Alex had gone into banking, real estate development, financing and brokerage. He had the Midas touch, and had he not been assassinated, he might easily have become the world's richest and most powerful man. But an evil cartel of power-crazed fanatics with the expressed purpose of taking over America had finally killed her father. Now, the Starbuck industrial empire remained for Jessica to own—or sell—as she chose. She chose to own and to expand.

She did not know exactly why. She needed no more money; it had long ago ceased to matter to her and she did not even know how much the Starbuck empire was actually worth. She ran it with the spirit of a hard-nosed business person, and yet it was really the vast army of employees that made it all worthwhile. And though Jessie would never have openly admitted as much, she took immense pride in the knowledge that her wealth had, in small but crucial instances, changed the course of developing nations for the better. Richer by far than small countries, she had had the unique luxury of playing a role in the course of world history. Her investments and the favorable terms of her loans had shored up more than one democracy, and conversely, her refusal to deal or service dictators had contributed to their fall.

The man across from her cleared his throat, attempting to attract attention to himself. He was probably accustomed to female attention, for he was a tall, strikingly handsome fellow with dark, wavy hair and light blue eyes. He did look hard-used, however. He was thin, his fingernails were broken, and he had the unmistakable air of a man who had ridden too many horses on too many backtrails. He wore a gun, and it appeared to Jessie that he was the kind of man who was very aware of that gun. He had introduced himself as

Buzz Ramsey, a New Mexico cattle rancher. Jessie didn't believe he was a rancher at all. *She* was a cattle rancher and she could spot another one in a minute by the cut of his clothes and the topics of his conversation. So far, Buzz Ramsey had not paid a moment's attention, either to the state of the range through which they passed or to the condition of the cattle they had seen. The man had no more interest in longhorn cattle than Jessie had in long-legged frogs.

"Miss Starbuck. I seem to have heard the name Starbuck before. Are you in banking, or what?"

She did not want to talk. It was too hot, the coach was too cramped, and the dust was thick. But she could not avoid a direct question and so she turned to look at Mr. Ramsey and the other passengers in the coach. Besides Ramsey, there was a widow named Mrs. Candace Whitman, who was also returning to Texas after journeying to bury her late husband who had died when he had suddenly taken ill in Albuquerque. Mrs. Whitman was a pretty woman in her mid-thirties with a tow-headed son about thirteen. The boy's name was Henry, and the death of his father had left him shaken and somber. She sympathized with young Henry; she had not been much older when her own father had suddenly died.

"Miss Starbuck?"

"Yes," Jessie said distractedly and with some annoyance, for she had just noticed that the Whitman woman looked very pale and faint.

"I asked if you were in banking."

She owned many banks, but chose to say, "I am mostly in cattle, as you said you were."

He raised his eyebrows and thumbed back his Stetson to reveal a wide, intelligent forehead and more of his curly brown hair. "Is that right?" he said with a big grin. "Well, how about that! And you being a woman. I'd never have guessed it. You look like the kind of woman who would own a millinery store or—to be honest, live in some big eastern city and work in a fancy place where rich people go."

Jessie said nothing.

The smile on his face died and he forced his next question. "Miss Starbuck, about how many cattle do you run?"

"A little over seventeen thousand."

His mouth actually fell open. "Ma'am, could it be that I really heard you correctly? Did you say 'seventeen thousand'?"

"Yes." Jessie ignored his amazement. She did not wish to be rude or abrupt, but the poor widow appeared ready to faint. "Mrs. Whitman, you look very peaked; shall I ask the driver to stop the coach?"

The woman shook her head. She was fragile looking, too fragile for this kind of travel. Jessie could tell at once that she was not strong and that the death of her husband had been the severest kind of blow. No doubt she was not left with a comfortable income, for her clothes and those of her sons were clean, but often mended.

Candace Whitman smiled and said, "No thank you, Miss Starbuck. Besides, I very seriously doubt the driver would stop on my account anyway." The reputation of stagecoach drivers as cantankerous and fiercely independent was well known throughout the West and accurate almost without exception.

"He will if I ask him to," Jessie said.

Deciding that she had better ask him, Jessie leaned her head out of the window and yelled, "Driver, please stop at that grove of cottonwood trees we will soon come to up ahead."

"You betcha, Miss Starbuck!"

"Well I'll be da—" Buzz Ramsey said, catching

himself before the ladies in time. "He actually is going to stop for you! What do you do, own this stageline or something?"

"Only a part of it, Mr. Ramsey. But the driver once worked for my outfit until cowboying became too rigorous. However, we are still friends."

Buzz shook his head. "You seem to carry a mighty wide loop in these parts. Is the Chinaman your servant, or what?"

Jessie looked at Ki. He betrayed no reaction, but she knew that he was offended by the racist and ignorant slight indirectly addressed to him. It happened all too often that stupid, unthinking men like Buzz Ramsey opened their mouths before they engaged their brains. Such men seemed to act as if anyone who was not white-skinned had no feelings or dignity. That made Jessie mad, and it showed when she said, "Not that it is any of your business, Mr. Ramsey, but Ki is my best friend, business advisor, and my . . . protector," she added, for it was the truth.

Jessie always carried a gun, and her father had taught her to use it, but Ki was a fighting man of the highest order. More than once, he had saved her life.

Ki turned to look at the man. "Mr. Ramsey," he said, "I am half Caucasian and half Japanese. My father was an American seaman and my mother comes from royal lineage. I am a samurai, and honor forbids me from taking action against the offense of being called Chinese."

Once again, Buzz Ramsey's jaw dropped. But after he had recovered, his smile stiffened a little and his blue eyes grew frosty. "Well, I'll be . . . derned," he said. "He *can* talk, and everything! And here I thought you were a mute or a mental deficient."

Ki blinked and Jessie reached out quickly and prevented him from rendering the insolent and totally unsuspecting Ramsey unconscious.

She said, "Ki, I think Mrs. Whitman will need our assistance in a few minutes. She has seen enough . . . unpleasantness. Don't you agree?"

Ki relaxed, looking almost ashamed of himself for even thinking about responding to the man across from them. "Of course. Were Hirata alive and with us, he would have been shamed by my thoughts."

"Who's Hirata?" Ramsey asked irritably.

Ki looked away. He would not soil his teacher's memory by sharing it with this crude ignoramus.

"I said, who is he?" Ramsey demanded with real heat in his voice.

Jessie had heard enough. "Mr. Ramsey," she said, her voice low but angry, "Hirata was Ki's teacher."

"Teacher of what? How to use chopsticks?"

Ki's hands knotted. He could kill this man with a single flick of his wrists. Send the steel-like edge of his hand forward to strike him at the base of the skull and break his neck. But the knowledge that it would be so easy made the samurai realize that self-control was his greatest strength, his most precious possession as given to him by his great samurai teacher. A samurai *never* lost control and struck out in anger. To do such a thing would be disgraceful.

Ki made himself grow peaceful inside, rejoicing in his inner strength and delighting in how he could test himself this day and prove he had not forgotten Hirata's greatest lessons—lessons greater by far than all the weapons of death that he had mastered, greater even than *te,* the art of empty-hand fighting in which a samurai's body becomes the ultimate weapon. For without inner strength and mental discipline, there was nothing but blind action and reaction—things no better than the lowest animal's instincts.

Jessie felt her samurai leaving them to journey down the soft, tranquil paths of his own mind. She breathed a deep sigh of relief, knowing she should not have

7

doubted that Ki would find it within himself to dismiss the insults for the emptiness they contained.

Jessie did not have such inner control, and she never would. She had no patience at all with someone like Ramsey and yet, wishing to avoid a confrontation in front of the pale woman across from her, she forced herself to explain. "Hirata was a *ronin*."

"Never heard of one of those," Ramsey said, attempting ridicule. "Is that somethin' like a roan horse, or what?"

Jessie flared angrily. "Are you interested in knowledge or only in making an even greater fool of yourself than you already have, Mr. Ramsey?"

He colored and the wind seemed to go out of his sails. "Reckon I have let the heat and the worry about Mrs. Whitman sort of get the best of me," he confessed. "Samurai, I apologize."

To prove it, he stuck out his hand. Ki took it, but without any real interest. To him, the man was simply there, a thing to be tolerated until their paths separated. Ramsey had no part of his *karma*, his life force, his past or his future.

"Now," Ramsey said, thinking that everything was fine and dandy, "what is a *ronin?*"

Candace said, "Yes, please tell us. I profess to be totally ignorant of Japanese customs. I'm sure that young Henry would also benefit from a little instruction, and it would help pass the time until we can stop and rest."

When Ki did not speak, Jessie took it to mean that she was free to answer. Besides, she sincerely believed that people could benefit from their knowledge of other cultures and customs. "Very well. In Japanese, *'ronin'* means a 'wave man,' one blown aimlessly like the waves of the ocean. Owning nothing, belonging to nothing, being nothing."

"Sounds kinda poor to me," Buzz Ramsey said.

"It is," Jessie agreed. "You see, a samurai is a Japanese warrior trained to protect his lord or master. Their entire lives are devoted to that single purpose. If they fail and their master is killed, they are expected to commit *seppuku*, which is ritual suicide."

"Oh dear," Mrs. Whitman said, looking even paler. "How terrible!"

"Yes," Jessie agreed. "But for a samurai, honor is life. Dishonor is death."

"How do they kill themselves?" Henry asked quietly.

"Henry!"

"I wanna know, Mother."

Jessie looked to Mrs. Whitman, thinking it might have been better not to have even mentioned *seppuku*. But she'd gone too far to quit now.

Mrs. Whitman apparently agreed. "I suppose that we need to know the truth, Miss Starbuck. Please answer my son's question, if you would be so kind."

"All right," Jessie took a deep breath. "*Seppuku* is ritual disembowelment. It is done with a short blade, using two long, deep cuts, one vertical, the other horizontal."

"I don't believe it!" Ramsey said, his handsome face a mixture of disgust and skepticism. "And I sure don't believe that you'd do that seppaka-whatchama-call-it to yourself, either!"

"The things you believe do not matter," Ki said quietly.

The insult was so quiet and yet so profoundly degrading that Ramsey started to reach for his sixgun. The samurai, not wishing to upset the other passengers, simply reached across the coach and dug his fingers into the base of Buzz Ramsey's thick neck. The man grunted softly, tried to lift his gun from his holster, then slumped forward unconscious.

"What did you do to him?" Henry cried.

"Nothing," Ki said, "except to apply pressure to one

9

of his pressure points. It shut off the supply of blood to his brain. But he will soon revive with no ill effects."

"Gosh!" The boy stared at Ki with awe. "What's that called?"

"*Atemi,*" the samurai replied.

"Will you teach me how to do it?"

Ki was about to say no, for such knowledge could be extremely dangerous, but Mrs. Whitman saved him the trouble. "Don't you dare!" she cried, pulling Buzz Ramsey up in his seat and holding him. "I don't want Henry to go around paralyzing other children."

"Of course not," Ki said. "But it seemed the easiest course of action to take at the moment."

"He may want to kill you when we stop. Miss Starbuck, all this talk has taken my mind off my misery. Can we just go on to the next stage-stop?"

Jessie nodded. "Of course." She again called up to the driver and gave him new instructions.

He relayed back that the next stop would be for dinner right about sundown at a place called Delgado's.

Jessie frowned. She had passed this way several times over the years and now she remembered that Delgado's was a rough stage-stop, frequented by even rougher men, many of them suspected outlaws. The food was bad, the overnight layover tense and unpleasant.

And there was Mr. Buzz Ramsey. He might just be a big enough fool to try and kill Ki. A young, handsome man who considered himself shamed before women and children might well be expected to do such a foolish and fatal thing.

Jessie sighed. It would be good to get back to her beloved Circle Star ranch.

★

Chapter 2

True to his word, the stagecoach driver arrived at Delgado's just as the sun was setting into the western horizon. The air quickly cooled and, as they disembarked, Jessie saw once again what a sleazy stage-stop this was, and decided that it ought to be burned to the ground and replaced. The problem was that old Ricardo Delgado owned all this rangeland. That meant that unless the line built a new stage road over several hills and across three major arroyos, Delgado's would remain the official stage-stop. It was a bad situation, and each year dozens of passengers were robbed or beaten—or worse—at this place.

Jessie was helped down by the driver, a man in his early fifties named Bob Belcher. He was a small, bandy-legged ex-cowpuncher who could have become a ranch hand but whose pride had been such that he could accept no other kind of ranch work except that which needed doing from the back of a horse. Jessie had tried to convince him that repair work around the headquarters was important, but Bob simply would have no part of it and scoffed at her offer as charity.

"Miss Starbuck," he said grimly as he surveyed the

11

corral of horses and listened to the rough laughter inside Delgado's, "it looks like we have a full house right now. You and Ki be careful in there. And if there's trouble, you know that I stand to help."

"That's appreciated," Jessie said, slapping the dust from her skirt. "I think that we'll sleep in the barn as usual."

"Probably a good idea. There's plenty of fresh straw in the loft and blankets, though it's too hot to have much use for 'em. You gonna ask the widow and her boy to join you?"

"Certainly."

Bob Belcher looked relieved. "This is sure a sorry danged place, isn't it?"

Jessie studied the low rock house and nodded. It was a large building with a pole- and dirt-covered roof. Twenty years ago, Comanches had trapped a band of ten buffalo hunters and hiders in this very place, and the men had staged a heroic stand against the huge Indian force. The siege had lasted two weeks, and three of the Texans had died attempting to reach the water well when they had gone mad with thirst. The others had survived mostly because Delgado's old rock house with its dirt roof was nearly impregnable.

Studying it now though, with its busted-out windows, piles of filth, flies, and a dirty blanket hanging where a door should have been, Jessie thought that Delgado's had seen its finest hour and ought to have been destroyed by the forces of nature.

"What about our friend?" Ki asked, motioning inside toward Buzz Ramsey.

"Let him sleep until the food is on the table," Jessie said. "Then I'll wake him up and try to talk him into being peaceable when he joins us to eat."

But Candace Whitman shook her head. She too was staring at the disreputable stage-stop and having second thoughts. "I think that Henry and I might sleep right here in the stagecoach," she said.

"Why don't you sleep in the barn with us?" Jessie asked. "I assure you it will be perfectly safe."

Bob Belcher said, "Ma'am, I'd sure advise you to accept that offer. I'll be sleeping up on the roof of this stage, but that don't mean that I could help you if there was sudden trouble. But the samurai can."

"I'd rather sleep in the stagecoach," Henry complained. "Can I stay here with Mr. Ramsey until he wakes up?"

"Why?" his mother asked.

Henry shrugged his shoulders. "Well, it's kind of a secret, but at the last stage-stop, he promised he would show me this little Indian carving he carries in his saddlebags which are tied on the roof. He said the carving was done by an old Apache medicine man and that it was a good luck charm. And he said I could have it if I wanted."

"He said that?" Mrs. Whitman looked dismayed.

"Yeah! Can I have it?"

"I guess so," the woman replied. "But I wish you wouldn't ask people for things."

"I *didn't* ask him for it; he just offered to give it to me!"

"All right," Candace said wearily. "I'll bring you out something to eat."

Henry beamed. It was the first smile that Jessie had seen on him, and it was a good one. She sort of liked the kid, and it seemed obvious to her that his mother and father had raised him to be well mannered and polite. Henry was tall for his age and wore glasses. He looked quite intelligent, and from the questions he had asked, Jessie suspected that he was.

"Why don't we all go inside and get the eating over with," Bob Belcher said, grabbing his shotgun and trooping off toward the rock house.

Ki let Mrs. Whitman and Jessie precede him across

13

the yard. He counted eight saddle-horses in the corral. It was good for a man to know what he faced beforehand.

"Ladies comin' in!" Bob Belcher yelled in the doorway. "Everybody inside better be dressed and watch their language for the ladies! No pickin' your noses or scratchin' where you oughtn't!"

Though Bob's warning was a little more explicit than Jessie would have preferred be given, it was not uncharacteristic. In the rugged, isolated parts of the West, such a warning was generally appreciated at the stage-stops. Most men on the frontier still treated women with respect; even the soiled doves that took their money working the cribs.

Still, Jessie felt her stomach tighten just a little as she moved into the dim interior of the stage-stop. There would be a few vulnerable moments before her eyes adjusted to the poor light; moments when she would be at a serious disadvantage.

Ki knew that too. That was the reason that he had closed his eyes as much as possible during the past hour. He had even done so as he had walked across the yard so that now, as he stepped inside, his vision was not seriously impaired. He saw ten men, eight of them eating at a long table with benches, and drinking whiskey from the bottle. Eight at the table, plus the cook and the bartender, whom he immediately dismissed as being of no consequence.

Because the eight had the look of outlaws and murderers, Ki started to touch Jessie on the arm to suggest that they remain outside and have the food brought to them, but it was too late.

"All right, you men," the stagecoach driver announced bravely. "This here is Mrs. Whitman and Miss Starbuck. You all have heard of the Starbucks of Texas and I can tell you both of these women are ladies and I won't tolerate any foolishness."

"Aw shut up," a big man with a hairy face roared.

"We kin see they is ladies! Good-lookin' ones, too!"

The other men laughed uproariously. Ki stepped out in front of Jessie. "Mr. Belcher asked that you men be polite. Now *I* will also ask you to show respect."

"Who the hell are you?" the same man shouted. "It'll be a sorry damned day that me or my friends will listen to a runty little Celestial bastard who—"

Ki moved so swiftly that no one really had time to react. One minute he was standing before Jessie; the next he was flying across the room and his fist was coming downward. It was a *tegatana* blow, perfectly delivered at the broad space between the big man's shoulderblades. The man grunted and his huge arms lifted toward the ceiling. Pain contorted his features and he seemed to be imploring God for mercy before he crashed over backward to the floor, groaning and writhing in agony.

The table emptied.

"Look out!" Jessie cried as a plateful of hot food was hurled to strike the samurai in the face. Scalding gravy and potatoes blinded the samurai, and he staggered. Jessie heard the shotgun explode toward the ceiling, knowing that Bob could not possibly risk firing into the melee without taking a chance of killing Ki as well as the men who were piling on him.

The samurai was borne down by their weight. He crashed to the floor and tried to fight back, but the weight on him pinned his arms to his sides.

Candace screamed and staggered backward. She whirled, then raced out the doorway. But Jessie threw herself on Ki's attackers with a vengeance. They were all big men, strong and brutal fighters, and they gouged and tore at the samurai, who could not get any punching or kicking room.

"Stop it!" Jessie cried, beating at the men, trying to rip them away from her friend.

Silver-haired Bob Belcher swore, reversed his shotgun, and knocked a man over with a mighty swing. But before he could raise the weapon to club another, he was kicked in the groin and sent to the floor. Helpless and in agony, he was also set upon.

When riding the range, Jessie carried a holstered gun. But when on business or wearing a skirt, she carried nothing more than a derringer. Now, she pulled it out of her skirt pocket and yelled, "Stop it or I'll kill—"

One of the men drew his gun and fired at her. Jessie ducked and used her bullet to send the man crashing over the table, dead before he hit the dirt floor.

But two of them pulled their own weapons, and one, a thin, weasel-faced man with a vicious knife-scar on his cheek, said, "Now, Miss Starbuck, let's just see how much of a lady you *really* are!"

He grabbed Jessie. She raked his eyes with her fingernails and he bellowed in pain. "You bitch!" he screamed. "I'll—"

Two gunshots filled the doorway. Tightly spaced, they each scored through the heart. The weasel-faced man stared at the expanding stain on his chest in amazement as the gun slipped from his numbing fingers. The other man just pitched over the table and died without a sound.

"Freeze!" Buzz Ramsey yelled.

But one man had his gun out, hidden. He cocked the weapon and lifted it.

"Look out!" Jessie cried.

Her desperate warning was enough. Ramsey twisted, threw himself sideways, and fired in one incredibly fast motion. Even so, he was wounded in the shoulder an instant before he unleashed two shots that caught the outlaw in the shirt pockets and punctured both lungs. The man screamed and collapsed in a frothy death. Buzz Ramsey's gun was instantly aimed at the last four men. "I load all six cylinders and I got three beans left to feed you bloody bastards," he said almost casually.

"So that means that one of you might live to walk out of here—but don't count on it. Now what's your choice, boys?"

Jessie stared at Buzz Ramsey with fascination, for she had never seen anyone who seemed cooler under fire, or more deadly. Had Ramsey yelled or ranted, done anything but smile that tight, terrible smile, he would not have seemed so murderous. But now, with a smile on his boyish good looks, and his bleeding shoulder, he appeared absolutely terrifying. Jessie had not realized it before, but Buzz Ramsey, for all his good looks, was a deadly man. A professional killer.

The four outlaws obviously reached the very same conclusion. They piled off Ki and backed up to the far wall, wearing expressions of abject fear.

"What are you going to do to us? Ain't you—"

"Shut up! Each one of you grab one of your dead friends and then march the hell outta here and don't look back. Say a word, make one false move, and you are buzzard bait. Hear me?"

"Yes sir!"

Jessie didn't wait to watch them being herded out to the corral and their horses. She was at the samurai's side. His face was already swelling and he was unconscious. Jessie jumped up and yelled to the cook and the bartender, who had wisely refrained from even moving during the fight. "Don't just stand there! Get me some water and a rag. Quickly!"

She hurried over beside Bob Belcher. He was on his knees, head down, gagging. Jessie had never seen any man kicked up between the legs the way this poor man had been kicked. "Bob, is there anything I can do?"

He shook his head. "Gettin'... gettin' too damned old and slow to fight," he groaned.

She placed her hand on his back in sympathy. "You tried," she said. "You risked your life for ours. That's important."

"How's the samurai?" he groaned.

Jessie returned to Ki. "He took a savage beating," she said. "As soon as you can drive again, we'll go on to Alder. Mrs. Whitman lives there and says the town has an excellent doctor."

"It's still a good hundred miles, and the horses are all played out."

"I know that. As soon as you're able, I want to push on anyway."

"Yes, ma'am."

He staggered to his feet and weaved toward the door. Jessie heard him retching outside. And then she heard something else—three quick gunshots and Candace Whitman's scream. Jessie grabbed the stagecoach driver's fallen shotgun. She jumped for the door, just in time to see one of the men with young Henry's neck locked in his forearm. The man's other hand was tugging at his vest and Jessie knew that he was reaching for a hideout gun.

Candace screamed again and Buzz Ramsey threw himself forward, despite his wounded shoulder. The two men staggered. Jessie watched hopelessly, knowing she could not fire. She saw the men and the boy crash to the earth. Then Buzz Ramsey was fighting for his and the boy's life. The outlaw got his hideout gun caught in the lining of his vest, and he cursed. Ramsey grabbed the weapon. They rolled over and over, and then there was a muffled gunshot.

Jessie held her breath.

Buzz Ramsey got up, but the outlaw beneath him stiffened. Then his lungs emptied themselves forever.

Candace grabbed her son and hugged him tightly. She was crying hysterically, but when Buzz staggered to his feet, she threw herself into his arms and sobbed on his good shoulder.

Jessie watched as Henry joined them. The boy's eyes

were shining with hero worship as he gazed up at Ramsey.

Jessie turned around and headed back to attend to the samurai. The scene of those three embracing in the stage yard should have brought joy to her heart, yet somehow it did not. Buzz Ramsey, if that was his real name, had killed seven hard men, and he'd done it much too efficiently. Granted, it had been absolutely necessary. But unless Ramsey was a famous lawman, Jessie had the feeling that Candace Whitman and her son were heading for big trouble if they trusted the tall stranger.

That was just a hunch, and not even a fair one, considering how the stranger had saved them all. But hunch, premonition, intuition, or whatever she chose to call it, Jessie was damned worried.

That worry did not subside when it came time to pull out. Ramsey had immediately laid claim to the outlaws' gear and horses. He had tied the string of eight horses onto the rear of the coach, and had thrown the dead men's saddles, bridles, and weapons on the roof. Even worse, when the man thought that no one was looking, Jessie had observed him emptying all the dead men's pockets.

That angered her so much, she privately confronted him and said, "I think you should leave everything."

"Why?" Ramsey asked, counting his newfound money and smiling with satisfaction. "The men who died won't be needing what belonged to them anymore. I killed those outlaws and they sure did need killing. Besides, it was a clear case of self-defense, wasn't it?"

"Certainly, but—"

"Listen," he said, growing serious, "you've already as much as told me that you are so rich you don't know how much you are worth, but I can sure tell you what I was worth when I rolled into this hellhole—about two dollars. Besides, after I sell all those horses and gear, I plan on giving some of the money to Mrs. Whitman. I get the feeling she could tell you exactly how much she is worth too."

Jessie felt stung. She also had to admit that there was some justifible anger in Buzz Ramsey. Maybe she was being unfair to criticize his actions as mercenary while in fact it was only sensible, given his and the widow's poor circumstances.

"I intended to offer her employment," Jessie said, knowing it sounded lame.

Ramsey raised his eyebrows. "Oh, how generous of you!" he said sarcastically. "Well, maybe she has a home and a town she wants to go on living in. Have you thought of that possibility?"

"She could refuse my offer."

"And she would," Ramsey said. "You aren't the only woman in Texas with a mess of pride."

Jessie flamed with anger. "What makes you think you can be such a judge of people? And what right do you have to presume anything about Mrs. Whitman?"

"None—yet." To inflame her even more, he had the audacity to wink.

Jessie left the man before she really lost her temper. She did not like Buzz Ramsey even if he had saved their lives!

A few minutes later she, Bob Belcher, and the two stageline employees carried Ki out to the stage and eased him across the cushions. He was breathing normally and his pulse was steady, but as yet he had not regained consciousness. His face was badly swollen and his eyes were blackened. She had seen Ki in many a battle, but never had he been beaten like this. Jessie knew that the samurai would never have let this happen if it had not been for her and Candace; he had deliberately not used weapons because a gunfight might have erupted and she could accidentally have been shot.

"Hey, Henry, you want to ride up here with me and the driver?" Ramsey called down to Henry.

The boy looked as if he were receiving a hand up to heaven from God. "Would I!" he shouted. "Could I?"

"Of course," Candace said. "Mr. Ramsey will watch out for you."

The boy scrambled up on top. A few moments later, the coach was rolling out of Delgado's.

For hours afterward, Candace Whitman talked. Jessica decided that it was a delayed reaction to the violence that had unleashed her tongue and her life story. She had often seen such a reaction from people who had just gone through a harrowing experience. Jessie learned that Candace's husband had been a cattle buyer, and that he had died on a business trip. He'd traveled a great deal, taking a small commission for bringing together cattle buyers and sellers.

"But my husband never really made a lot of money," she confided. "He was always . . . well, he was a gambler. It was his only vice. But if we got half of what he really made, I always considered ourselves fortunate. He was, despite that one serious fault, a very fine father and husband."

"It shows in Henry," Jessie said. "You have done a good job with the boy. I just, um, just sort of hope that the boy learns to be a little more questioning about strangers."

Candace frowned. "What do you mean by that?" Her tone had a definite edge. She *knew* what Jessie meant.

"I just don't want to see either you or the boy hurt again," Jessie said. "I think you should be careful about strangers."

"Miss Starbuck! You are referring to the man that saved all of our lives, aren't you?"

"Yes," she said patiently. "And I am no less grateful than you are, but—"

"Miss Starbuck!" Even in the faint moonlight that

penetrated the coach, it was plain to see that the widow was extremely upset. "Miss Starbuck, I have invited Mr. Ramsey to live with myself, Henry, and my mother in our house until such time as he is sufficiently recovered from that gunshot wound which he took saving *our* lives!"

Jessie sighed. She could tell that there was no good purpose in continuing with her warning about Buzz Ramsey. It was painfully clear that the widow had either fallen in love with the stranger or fully intended to allow herself to do so.

"Of course you're right," Jessie said, hoping to smooth the poor woman's ruffled feathers. "And that is a very charitable thing to do. I did not realize that your mother was staying with you. But either way, I would like to offer you, her, and Henry the hospitality of my Circle Star ranch. We even have several small but comfortable guest houses that you would find very suitable. I could use some help."

Candace was thrown off balance. "You need *my* help?"

"Of course. I think we could be friends. Henry would be tutored privately—as are all of the children who live on our ranch—and he would be quite happy."

Candace shook her head softly. "I'm ashamed of myself for the way I've just spoken. Here I was, angry and . . . and, yes, very jealous. And there you are, trying to help me and Henry."

Jessie reached across the coach. She liked this woman very much. And though Candace Whitman's world probably had very little in common with her own, Jessie knew that they could be good friends. Her own mother had died early on, and Jessie had often wished she had an older sister to confide in. Maybe Candace could fill a longstanding void in her life, Jessie thought.

* * *

Ki awoke long after midnight and listened to the two women talking. The fact that they were alive and obviously in good health was a refreshment to his troubled spirit. He had failed to protect Jessie from danger, though he had managed to divert its focus from her to himself. Still, he had failed, and it had been required that Mr. Ramsey save the boy and two women from certain harm.

Ki considered what he had done and what he should have done, in case the need ever arose again. He should, he supposed, have entered the station before Jessie and then asked that the outlaws show respect. When they refused, he could have acted with however much force would have been required.

Still, Ki knew that he was only mortal, despite the fact that his amazing weapons and skills seemed nearly unbelievable to those who did not know or understand *te* or the use of such weapons as the bow, the staff, the *surushin* of his deadly star-blades, the *shuriken*. But despite those skills and weapons, he was unmistakably fallible. He could be overwhelmed, and he could be rendered helpless, as he had been at Delgado's.

Such a realization did not dismay him, but instead made him more resolved to use greater intelligence with his fighting skills. He must never place himself into such a position as to be overwhelmed again. The stakes were Jessica Starbuck's life, and they were much too high.

In the darkness, he reached down and touched his side, knowing that his entire ribcage was smashed. He counted nine broken or cracked ribs. Those men had methodically slammed their knees into his face and sides with murderous intent. Ki supposed he ought to feel fortunte that it was not his *karma* to have his lungs punctured, which would most certainly have resulted in his death.

But he did not feel fortunate at all. The only good thing that he could think of was that he and Jessica were returning to Circle Star, where he could rest, feeling assured that she was among her friends and in complete safety until he could travel, again confident of being able to protect her.

The samurai closed his mind to his own physical pain and rested, knowing that the new day would bring a doctor, who would examine him and then confirm his own diagnosis.

He tried to think of tranquil things, but found that his unruly mind was nagged by the same fears that Jessica had expressed by the way she had treated the supposed cattle rancher. Namely, that, despite Mr. Ramsey's extraordinary ability with a handgun, there was something very menacing about him, something that did not ring true. Jessica's intuitions about people were every bit as sharp as his own, and as usual, they were in perfect accord.

Without any doubt, Mrs. Candace Whitman and her young son were to be used by the pale-eyed gunfighter. But for what purpose? They had little money.

It was a mystery, and the samurai loved mystery. But this was one that he would not have the luxury of solving. Not from a bed at Circle Star. Not with a chest full of broken ribs.

The doctor finished his examination and shook his head. He turned to Jessica and said, "Miss Starbuck, my advice is that he might very well have a bone fragment come loose and puncture his lungs if he is moved a single inch. I suggest he remain right here, where I will give him around-the-clock medical care."

Jessie glanced at the samurai who shook his head once. She knew that Ki would never consent to being left behind. "I'm sorry," she told the doctor. "He rode a rough stagecoach over a hundred miles, and it is only another hundred to my ranch. I will take the chance."

"And if he dies, will you be capable of handling your guilt?"

Ki's eyes narrowed and his voice was weak but left no doubt as to his displeasure. "It is *my* life to live as I choose. Besides, if a bone was going to puncture a lung it would have done so long before now," he said, angered that the doctor would say such a stupid thing in order to increase his fees, which he would probably double in Jessica's case because of her well-known wealth.

To prove his point, Ki sat up and then eased off the examination table to stand.

"My God!" the doctor cried. "You have no business being on your feet!"

Jesssie came over, and the samurai allowed her to assist him to the coach. The pain in his chest was so overpowering, he thought that he might not be able to reach the door, much less climb into the coach.

But he did. And when he was finally at rest, he found he was weak and breathing rapidly. Mrs. Whitman and young Henry were there to bid them farewell, but Mr. Ramsey was conspicuous by his absence.

Ki heard Jessica reiterate her offer of employment and assistance, but the attractive widow declined. That was unfortunate. Ki would have liked to have taught the boy a few things, and the woman seemed as if she could use the help. Ki wondered if Mrs. Whitman would have declined if it had not been for Mr. Ramsey. Perhaps the man had already left her and she would soon be arriving at Circle Star for a long visit.

Jessie hugged the pair goodbye and then climbed back into the coach. Bob Belcher was going to drive them directly to Circle Star headquarters. Ki was grateful. He had not realized that nine broken ribs could prove so troublesome.

★

Chapter 3

Buzz Ramsey had watched the stagecoach leave Alder, relieved to see it go. He had seen Jessica Starbuck hug Candace Whitman and knew that she had offered the widow employment and a place to stay.

Buzz had resented that. All his life he had been interested in accumulating great wealth, and now, at the age of thirty-two, he knew that it would not happen for him. Except for a few rare incidents where men had discovered gold or claimed an empire of grass when it was still freely available, Buzz knew that men did not get rich without being born into money or at least having access to powerful friends.

Buzz had neither. His father had been a Nebraska sodbuster, a man who had fought the weather, the soil, bad crop prices, grasshoppers, and pestilence until it had broken his will and his spirit. Buzz had been the fourth son of Eachem Morris, and had never known a day of his childhood that he had not worked from nearly sunup to sundown. But then, when he was sixteen, a traveling drummer had come by and Buzz had run away. The drummer's name had been Rufus Ramsey and he had, in his youth, been a gunfighter of considerable note. In the years that followed, Rufus had taught Buzz all the tricks of a professional gunman and cardsharp. He had sworn that, if a man knew how to cheat at cards and defend himself when caught—as he would most certainly be once in a while—then he could survive and live in high style. Old Rafe had shown Buzz many a daguerreotype of himself with lovely women perched on his lap in his wild and prosperous days. Rafe had spent his best days as a Mississippi riverboat gambler, and he had spoken of winning thousands of dollars in a single night. Buzz had believed him, and knew it was the truth when the old drummer had bragged that he had enjoyed more women and liquor than six normal men.

Buzz had loved and admired the old drummer, and when Rafe had been shot and killed for the small change in his pockets, Buzz had hunted down the murderers and gunned them down in a blazing battle. It had been a bittersweet victory, that first blood spilled. Rafe had always told him that, no matter how good a man was with a gun during practice, the moment of truth came only in a real fight. Buzz had survived his "moment of truth" over and over during his years as a bounty hunter, occasional outlaw, and even a lawman once when very broke and on a streak of bad luck with both cards and ladies. When he had left Albuquerque on the run from the law, he had adopted Rafe's last name. Not only would this give him a new chance to finally go straight, but he had always intended to change his last name anyway because Ramsey meant something more to him than his own sodbuster father who had worn himself out in Nebraska.

Now, however, he was at the midterm of his life, and thinking that he might be wise to settle down and find steady employment. During the long stagecoach ride into Texas, he had tried to charm Jessica Starbuck but quickly realized she was too far out of his reach. Candace Whitman, however, was very accessible and at a point in her life when she needed the services and strength of a man. So he had switched his attention to the widow and found that she was completely vulnerable to his not inconsiderable charms. And during the last twenty-four hours, Buzz had come to understand that she was his key to a better life—she had respectability and she owned a house. Besides, Buzz liked young Henry. Although it was certainly possible, Buzz did not believe he had sired any children, but if he had, Henry was the kind of boy he would have wished for as a son.

So as the stagecoach pulled out, Buzz figured that he might try and establish himself here in Alder. He also might marry Candace and adopt young Henry and teach him a few card tricks and how to draw and fire a sixgun.

But there was a major problem. Because he had stepped across the line and robbed a few men and banks in Wyoming, Montana, and Colorado, there could be men down in this part of the country who recognized him from an old Wanted poster issued in Denver for extortion and murder. Two years before, he had tried to extort funds from a Denver banker, and when the man had hired a professional gunman to protect himself and his funds, Buzz had killed them both in a standup fight that Buzz considered self-defense.

With its thousand-dollar reward, the Wanted poster had dogged him ever since. Having worked as a bounty hunter himself, he knew the kind of men who would be attracted by a reward of that size. It caused him much loss of sleep, and his hand was never far from his gun. But if he married Candace, changed his last name from Ramsey to Morris, and took up some humdrum job in a little Texas town like this one, Buzz figured he might finally shed his past. As much as he had hated being the son of a sodbuster, sometimes he thought that being a man on the run was even worse. And he had never been able to get a good explanation out of old Rafe as to why, if he had made all that money, he had ended up driving a run-down peddler's wagon and selling snake oil and liniment to old sick people.

When the stagecoach rounded a bend and disappeared, Buzz moved too quickly and was punished with a very sharp pain in his wounded shoulder. He had been mighty lucky to kill seven men and only get himself winged. And in doing so, he won the heartfelt gratitude and hospitality of the widow and her boy. It had all worked out rather neatly. All that was required was to give Candace a few weeks to mourn her late husband, and then marry the attractive woman. Oh yeah, and find some work that would be both interesting and make some good money.

"Mr. Ramsey?"

He turned to see Henry staring at him. "Yeah?"

"My mother wants you to come meet my grandma and settle in."

Buzz nodded. He would charm the old buzzard silly until the wedding date, and then he would boot her the hell out of his new house.

Six months later, he was to remember his prediction with a wry grin. He had underestimated the opposition. Candace had indeed fallen in love with him and wanted to marry, yet propriety and some stupid sense of etiquette had made her resolve not to marry for at least one year from the date of her late husband's death.

Buzz had almost quit his job at the telegraph office and taken up the wild life again. Working every day from morning to night and having to take orders while doing it was the hardest thing he had ever attempted. Almost a hundred times he had decided to quit and then, at the very last minute, changed his mind.

Why? Buzz had to admit that he had also fallen in love with Candace and he wanted the boy to be his son. It was that simple, and he was enough of a man to admit as much to himself. The worst part of it, though, was that he couldn't stand his future mother-in-law, and she openly detested him. The lady was sharp and suspicious. She did not think that Buzz was worth being her daughter's husband and said so at every opportunity. Buzz would have liked to toss the old bag out in the street, for he was certain that it was the mother who had planted that stupid idea about a one-year mourning period.

There were other flies in the ointment. He and Henry had to sneak out of town so that he could teach the kid to draw and fire a sixgun. Teach him how to deal a deck from the bottom and mark cards with his thumbnail so skillfully they could only be seen by holding them up to the light. Henry had talent with both the gun and the cards. He was still clumsy and lacked confidence, but he would become very good if he kept practicing alone at night in his bedroom.

"Aren't you finished sending that telegram yet?" Edward Holmes said angrily. "Buzz, the problem with you is that you daydream too damn much. I want to help you make this your life's work, but you sure aren't taking hold very good. I got three men younger and quicker than you who are just waiting for me to fire you."

"Then maybe you should," Buzz said, for he had taken more than enough from Holmes and the thought of sending telegrams for the next forty years was not much more appealing than the thought of following a plow up and down the endless rows of a cornfield.

Mr. Holmes looked pained. He was a fat man with bad eyes and worse breath. "You know how fond everyone in Alder is of Mrs. Whitman. If I fired you, why, I'd be made to look like a damned ogre. But you are slow to learn and even slower to send messages."

Buzz clenched his teeth. He was too damned old to be sitting here doing a boy's work. Sure he was slow, but that was because the job was so boring his mind kept wandering off to better times. To other women and towns and card games that . . .

"Well, go ahead and send the goddamn thing!" Holmes shrieked.

Buzz leaned forward and forced himself to concentrate on the message before him. He touched the telegraph keys, concentrating on the Morse code. And slowly, almost painfully, his long, supple gambler's fingers clumsily played out another boring message from the local store to a big St. Louis supply house. The telegraph would run three pages, and was nothing more or less than an elaborate shopping list.

It was enough to drive a sane man to drink. He was still thinking that when, late that afternoon, two men walked into the telegraph office to send a message. The moment Buzz saw them, he knew they were professional bounty hunters, and when they gave him a second glance, and then a third, he knew that somewhere in the dim recesses of their memories they had seen his Wanted posters and were trying to remember the charge and the bounty.

Because looking away would only have heightened their suspicions, Buzz played the bumpkin, the cloying fool. Seeing Mr. Holmes's spectacles lying nearby, he picked them up and peered myopically at the two hardcases.

"Well good day, gentlemen," he said almost breathlessly. "Can I help you?"

The two men studied him coldly. "Where do you hail from?" one asked him bluntly.

"Right here in Alder." Buzz feigned confusion. "Why, do I . . . do I know either of you gentlemen?"

They exchanged glances. "You ever been to Denver?"

"Why no, sir! But I'd like to someday." He smiled widely. "I sure send a good many telegrams to that fine city by the mountains."

Apparently satisfied for the moment, the taller of the two pulled out his money and said, "Send this telegram to the U.S. Marshal in Miles City, Montana."

"Yes, sir! Message reads, 'Have killed three members of the Waco Gang. Names are Billy Beamon, Tom Radney, and Elvin Putter. Rewards are a hundred dollars each. Confirm with sheriff of Alder, Texas, and send three hundred dollars reward money pronto. Signed, Micah and Josh Slade.'"

"All right, so you proved you can read. Send the damn message!"

"Yes, sir!"

Buzz had to steady himself as he tapped the message across the lines. The Waco brothers were known to be treacherous and fast on the trigger. If these two men had killed them, they had to be very, very good. Buzz did not want to arouse their suspicions as he began to tap out their message. Of course, the Slades would not know if he was sending their message correctly or not, and that was a good thing because he knew he was making a good many mistakes. Even so, he went right through the telegram, one eye on the paper, the other on his hand.

"What's your name, mister?"

Buzz looked up, the picture of innocence. "Bill Ramsey."

"You ever been in Wyoming or Montana?"

"No, sir. I'm afraid I'm not a very adventuresome sort. Born and raised right here."

"You sure look adventuresome enough to do more than play pitty-fingers with a damn telegraph key. A big man like you ought do a man's work."

Buzz coughed, then said, "Please, that will be two dollars, gentlemen."

They paid him and started to walk out. But then, one of them turned and said, "Did you say you been in this hick town all your life?"

"Yes."

"Then I guess you're not the man that we were thinking you might be."

They slammed the door on their way out. Buzz relaxed for a moment, and then he sat bolt upright. The Slade brothers were heading straight for the sheriff's office, and if they came out again real quick, Buzz knew that would mean they had asked the sheriff if Bill Ramsey, the telegraph operator, was a homegrown boy. Of course, the sheriff would tell them his real name was *Buzz* Ramsey and that he had been in town only six months after gunning down seven men at old Ricardo Delgado's stage-stop.

Buzz held his breath. He could feel his heart pounding as he stared at the window and waited to see what would happen. He tried to tell himself that he had fooled the Slade brothers because his act was so convincing. But he didn't believe it. A pair of veteran bounty hunters were not so easily fooled—even by one of their own kind.

Five minutes later, he saw the door of the sheriff's office open, and then the Slade brothers stepped outside. They were smiling and looking down the street as if they had nothing important on their minds. It was an act. An act that Buzz knew well and had performed dozens of times just as convincingly in order not to arouse the suspicions of the local sheriff. If you did that, he'd demand to be in on the arrest or shooting and thus earn himself half of the bounty. Small-town sheriffs were hungry bastards. They could smell a bounty, and unless the Slades were very casual, their questions would arouse suspicion.

The Slades checked their guns and moseyed down the street. Twice, they erred by glancing at the telegraph office, and that was more than enough for Buzz. He stood up and removed the flimsy uniform jacket that

Holmes required of his employees. He rolled down his sleeves over his muscular forearms and reached for the sixgun he carried in his jacket pocket.

"Hey! What are you doing!" Holmes snapped, coming in from the back room, where he had been doing some of his weekly reports. "Put that uniform jacket back on or—"

Buzz didn't wait for him to finish. He shoved his sixgun in the man's fat gut and thumbed back the hammer. Holmes's reaction was as instantaneous and dramatic as Buzz could have wished. His mouth widened in a silent scream of fear. His red, runny little eyes dilated and the rosiness bled from his plump cheeks.

"How would you like me to blow a couple of holes through all this suet and let some of it drain out on the floor?" Buzz asked quietly.

The fat man shook his head violently. His sagging cheeks wagged. "Oh, please, I didn't mean to rush you, Buzz," he begged. "I'd never fire you. Honest!"

"If you didn't have a wife and children to support, I think I would pull the trigger, you bossy, foul-breathed little parasite."

Buzz eased up on the hammer. Then he shoved the sixgun into his waistband while his ex-boss watched him buttoning his heavy coat. The moment the gun was out of sight, Holmes seemed to regain his backbone.

"Why you . . . How dare you pull a gun on me! You're fired, and I mean to have you arrested!"

Something snapped in Buzz. For months, he had been forced to bow and scrape to this pompous toad for the privilege of earning even less money than he had earned as Rufus Ramsey's sales assistant. And now . . . now it all came down to stand for nothing. His hard work and the safe world he had tried to construct had crashed to his feet the moment that Micah and Josh Slade plowed through the door.

Buzz stepped back, cocked his fist, and sent it crashing into the middle of the man's face. He laughed to feel Holmes's porcine snout crumple under his knuckles, and when the man squealed like the pig he was, Buzz whistled a short uppercut to his chin that lifted him off the ground and sent him sprawling across the desk, ripping the telegraph key from its wires.

"I guess *you* got the goddamn message this time. No charge," he snarled, turning on his heel and heading for the front door.

He slammed it hard and headed off to ask Candace and Henry to go away with him—or at least to wait until he could send for her after he made some real money. A few big games at the tables, maybe even a small bank job or two, and he would set them up for keeps.

Candace Whitman sat on her porch at twilight, shaken to the core, her hands clenched. "You could give yourself up," she said. "Just turn yourself over to the sheriff before the bounty hunters come."

"No," he said, both to her and to Henry, who sat watching him quietly. "You see, once they had me in the pokey, they'd start investigating a little and discover some of the other jobs that I did outside of Colorado."

"There were others!"

"Candace, listen to me. All my life I've been wanting to make one really big pile of money and then go straight. If you and Henry wait for me, I'll do it this time and—"

Her eyes blazed. "Do you think I could live with a man who had gotten his money from robbing banks! Never!"

Buzz took a deep breath. "Then I guess this is goodbye," he said. "At least you'll have to admit I was honest with you."

Her face didn't soften. "You were *finally* honest because you had no choice. Tell me, was it your intention to get married and then let me find out someday about your past? Someday, when another bounty hunter stumbled across you and recognized your face?"

"I thought . . . I never thought it would happen," he said lamely. "You see, a man with a reputation with cards and a gun doesn't usually love someone enough to grovel in a telegraph office for small change. I'd never have expected to find a bank robber working at a telegrapher's desk."

Candace raised her chin. "Mother said there was a streak of danger in you one mile wide. And also deception. She was right. I should have known that when it became apparent that you had no cattle ranch in New Mexico. Not that it mattered; I'd have loved you poor as well."

"Mother! He just told us the truth. We got to help him now!"

"No!" she cried. "He saved us once. We have given him shelter, food and . . . and our love. But he has tricked us. We owe him nothing."

Buzz shook his head. He stood up. "I guess I'll go pack my bag and head on out before they come gunning."

"Please do," she told him. "I have seen enough death."

"Henry. You need the example of a man. I want you to come with me."

"No!" Candace cried, jumping up and grabbing her boy. "Mr. Ramsey, you are most certainly not the kind of example that I want for my son!"

"I was doing fine until this afternoon," he said. "Henry turned fourteen last week and he's as tall as a man. When I was his age, I left the farm. There is a big world out there to see, and he's ready."

"Get out of here!" she cried.

"Henry, you're old enough to make up your own mind now."

The boy wavered. It was plain to Buzz that he wanted to go.

"I can't leave my mother."

Buzz hid his disappointment as best he could. "All right," he said, sticking out his hand. "Good luck."

"Where will you be going?" Henry asked.

"Better that I not say."

"They'd have to kill me before I talked!"

Buzz smiled. He knew that it was the truth, and he was proud of Henry. "I know that. You don't forget to practice with that deck of cards and that gun I gave you, remember?"

"I will."

"You gave my son cards and a pistol?"

"Yeah," he said to her. "I did. Better he learns from me than from somebody who'd take advantage of his ignorance, and either cost him his life or his fortune."

"Get off my property!"

Buzz grabbed her by the shoulders and kissed her hard. She struggled and then clung to him, and he knew for sure that she had loved him. He could taste the salty tears that ran down her cheeks, and it filled him with sorrow. He pushed her away and turned to leave, knowing that he could not bear to say another word.

He was moving down the stone path between her flower garden and the vegetable garden when the Slade brothers opened up from across the street. Buzz felt a bullet spin him like a top. He reached for the gun, now resting on his hip, and his arm would not do his bidding. He crashed into the fallow garden and rolled twice as more gunfire sounded and the Slades came dashing across the street. He heard Candace yelling for help; then he managed to reach around with his left hand and pull his gun from its holster.

They figured he was dead or dying, but he was about to prove them dead wrong. Buzz yanked his gun out with his left hand and, as the first bounty hunter came bursting through the picket gate, he drilled him twice through the chest. Old Rafe Ramsey had made him learn to shoot straight with either hand. The man screamed and was knocked back into his brother. They disappeared from view, but Buzz knew that the second bounty hunter was close.

Then he heard the man.

"You kilt my brother, goddamn you!" he screamed. "And even if you get me they'll be others in my family that'll come gunnin' for you! You're a dead man either way!"

Buzz thought he saw the man, and triggered two shots—only they both misfired. He pulled the trigger again, but the hammer of the gun was stuck. In the rapidly fading light, Buzz realized that he had slammed the gun down hard to break his fall and when he had landed in the garden, it had become fouled with dirt. In good light, with thirty seconds, he probably could have fixed the problem.

But he didn't have good light, and he would be dead in thirty seconds. He frantically began to crab backward toward the house. Behind him he heard the door slam. Then Candace shouted, "Henry, no!"

Slade was coming. Sick with grief and wild with the need to avenge the death of his brother, he rose to his feet and raced down the outside of the fence to the end of the property. Then he vaulted it and came in with his sixgun blazing. His first shot was far wide; his second much closer. Buzz tried to whirl and run, but he stumbled in the soft garden dirt and fell sprawling. He twisted, tossed his useless gun aside, and prepared to meet death face to face, like a man.

Slade halted not ten feet away. His face was contorted with rage. But now, seeing his man helpless, he laughed wickedly and said, "You murderin' son of a bitch, the poster says dead or alive and—"

A single shot filled the yard, and Slade popped up on the very tips of his toes. He staggered around toward the porch and struggled with his last bit of strength to raise his gun. Henry Whitman shot him again. This time, Slade went down for good.

Buzz climbed to his feet and swatted the dirt off his clothes. He examined the ragged hole and the blood from the wound in his right forearm. When he looked up, he saw neighbors standing on their porch, staring. The entire neighborhood was coming out. In a few minutes, so would the sheriff. Buzz did not want to stick around and be forced to kill the man.

"I better leave, pronto."

"I'm coming with you," Henry said. "With that arm, you wouldn't stand a chance alone. Not for long, at least."

"That's true enough, but what about your mother?"

"I'm a man now; I reckon sticking with you is better than living in a house with two women. We better hurry."

He clapped the boy on the shoulder and turned to see Candace blocking his path. "You'll lead him to a gallows, Buzz Ramsey—or whoever you are. A gallows or a bullet before he is twenty, I'll bet."

"We'll come back for you someday," he told her, not wanting to fight and not having the time for it anyway. "In the meantime, you and your mother go to Circle Star and you'll be safe from their kinfolk."

"This is my home."

"I know those kind of men," Buzz said. "You *have* to leave. They won't care that you're a woman and that you had nothing to do with this. Your son killed one of them, and the man you love killed the other."

"The man I thought I loved never existed," she told him in a voice devoid of all emotion.

Buzz wanted to shake her into her senses. "Candace, you must promise me you'll ask Miss Starbuck for help and protection! Promise me that and I promise I'll bring Henry back someday!"

She finally nodded. "I'll write to her at Circle Star."

Then she walked back into the house and shut them both out of her life.

★

Chapter 4

Jessie waited until the Circle Star cook and his Mexican helper had finished bringing in the huge platters of steaks, potatoes, and carrots stewed in wine and a special sweet sauce.

"It looks magnificent!" the Argentine rancher said, his English almost flawless. Dante Manalos was a tall and broad-shouldered man in his early thirties. He was handsome and bold enough to have been an actor. "I have always heard that longhorn beef is tough."

Jessie smiled. "It can be," she said, amused by his frankness. "But if it is prepared correctly, it can be cut with the edge of your fork."

"Oh?" He raised his eyebrows questioningly.

"Try it," she said.

He did, and it made him smile. He speared a morsel and ate it with great enjoyment. Then he nodded to Jessie and said, "You win—this is magnificent beef!"

Jessie winked at Dante. "I have a confession to make."

He stopped chewing and pretended to be alarmed. "Don't tell me you have fed me dog or something!"

"No," she said. "It's just that our steaks are not entirely longhorn. For the past few years, I've been cross-breeding some Hereford blood into our herds."

"Those red and white English cattle?"

"Yes. I have discovered that about a quarter of their blood gives us a better beef animal, one built with more flavor and tenderness."

"Now you have told me your secret, Jessica! I will return to Argentina and buy some of those cattle to crossbreed with our own native animals."

"Better yet," Jessie said, "why not buy the product of five years of scientific breeding directly from Circle Star?"

"You would do this?" The Argentine seemed genuinely surprised.

"Yes," Jessie said, "but there are strings attached to the price."

"Oh," Dante said, "now we get down to it. All right, how much will these special-breed cows and bulls cost me?"

"Five thousand for each bull. A thousand for each heifer. I'll pay the sea-fare."

"And why shouldn't you—you own a fleet of ships!" he cried, half laughing and half serious. "Still, you're price is pretty high. I would need a hundred bulls minimum, and five times that many heifers."

"You can afford it. Now, take another bite," Jessie said, "and I'll tell you about the strings that I intend to attach."

The Argentine looked at her closely, his dark eyes frank and appraising. "You are as tough a businessman as your father, Jessica."

"Thank you. But it's 'businesswoman'."

He nodded and raised his glass of champagne to her. His eyes made love to her face and breasts. "Of course, only a man one hundred years old or blind could fail to see that. I think you are the most beautiful woman I have ever seen. And the most appealing."

44

"Even more than Princess Lidia, who you courted in Europe last year?"

He swallowed his wine quickly. "Oh, you heard about that, did you?"

"All of Europe heard," Jessie said. "Lidia has often been called the most beautiful woman in the world."

"Ha! Whoever said that has not seen you." Dante smiled roguishly. "Besides, it was she that left me."

Jessica liked that. Many men would have bragged about leaving the woman; this one lied—but to protect her reputation instead of his own. "That's not true, Dante. I received a letter from the princess just last week, and she told me that you broke her heart. She said she wanted to marry you."

Dante gulped his champagne and tried to look crestfallen. "Dear Jessica," he said, "the sad truth is that I was not worthy of her. Nor am I of you. I admit this all takes me by surprise. I did not know you and she were close friends."

Jessie ate her food slowly and reached her decision. She had been told by her man in Argentina that Dante was honorable; now she was sure and ready to proceed. "Aren't you curious about the strings that I mentioned?"

He nodded. "You will tell me when you choose."

"I choose to do so now. Your country needs a new railroad system. Your president agrees, and has ordered the surveying work to begin next month. The system is to be over two thousand miles in length. I want a chance to bid for delivery of the rails."

"Ah," he said, setting his fork down and studying her closely. "You want me to intercede on behalf of your Starbuck Enterprises and win you the contract."

"No," Jessie said, "not quite. I want you to do the bidding for me. Be my representative in Argentina. I want you to win the contract, but do so fairly. I will beat anyone's price, and at the highest quality. Dante, the rails that you already have used to date have come from

45

Russia. They are inferior. They have caused a number of train derailments and will not last more than three years. It is because of the poor smelting process and iron ore the Russians are using. I think that Argentina and its citizens deserve the best railroad that money can buy. Don't you?"

He was truly astonished by her knowledge. "And you really want me to bid fairly? If that is it, why not have one of your men do it?"

"Because there are high-ranking figures in the Argentine government who are on the take, who profit by making deals for inferior goods at higher prices. An American employed by the Starbuck empire wouldn't stand a chance at being fairly treated. But a native Argentine, a man as famous and respected as you are—that is another story."

"Perhaps you give me too much credit," he said. "I am no friend of the president's."

"I know that, but the people respect you. It will not be easy, Dante. You may put your life in danger."

He sighed. "How did you learn so much about corruption in my government?"

"I make it a point to know such things. I also know who is honest and who is not. You are one of the few wealthy and influential men who have consistently refused to turn your head to graft and dishonesty in Argentina. Despite the personal danger this places you in, you continue to be outspoken against corruption."

He bowed his head slightly. "Thank you. I am flattered. Of course I will do this—for you, and for my fellow countrymen. You will, of course, enjoy a profit."

"Of course. Always a profit, but one fairly earned, Dante."

"That is only fair. *But,*" he said, emphasizing the word heavily, "*I* have a string that I desire to attach."

Jessie waited, not sure what to expect. Dante was

rich; he was too honorable to quibble over the price of the cattle, and she suspected that he would have done her bidding for the railroad contract simply because it would benefit his countrymen. "Then ask whatever you like," she told the handsome Argentine, "and if it is within my power to do so, it will be yours."

"I want to make love to you right now," he said, without batting an eye. "Right here on this tablecloth before that great fireplace."

She was shocked, but recovered quickly and then could not help but laugh. "The princess told me that you were totally without principles when it came to making love. She said you enjoyed having a woman in the most unusual places."

"I confess it is true," he said, sounding contrite, but thoroughly enjoying himself.

Jessie pushed her plate aside. She had suddenly lost her appetite. She raised her glass and drank, her eyes frank and appraising. "Did you really make love to her on top of a Belgian horse?"

"She admitted that?" He covered his face in mock embarrassment and groaned.

"Yes. She said..." Jessica giggled softly at the image. "She said that after you and she were... together, you made the huge draft animal trot."

He threw his head back and roared. "Oh yes!" he cried. "And it was wonderful until we fell off the damned clumsy beast. Had I not slipped out on the way down, I might have seriously injured her, and myself!"

They both laughed until tears steamed down their faces. But then, when the laughter stopped, Jessica rose from her chair and called for the cook and his helper. "Leave the champagne and glasses," she told them, "and throw a few extra logs on the fire. Mr. Manalos and I have to talk business late tonight. Under no circumstances whatsoever do we wish to be disturbed."

"Not even by Ki? He had a letter he wished to speak to you about. He said it was important."

"Do you know who it was from?"

"No, Miss Starbuck."

"Whatever it was, it can wait until morning. Thank you for the fine dinner."

"It was magnificent!" Dante said.

The cook beamed. "But what about dessert, Miss Starbuck?"

She glanced at Dante and he smiled, his eyes dancing in the firelight. "We will have our dessert . . . later."

"Very good, Miss Starbuck. Just ring when you are ready. I'll be in the kitchen waiting."

She took the cook's arm and ushered him out, saying, "Go to bed, Fredrick. Just leave the dessert on the table and we will help ourselves later."

"Very good," he said, pleased that he could leave. "Good night, ma'am, Mr. Manalos."

The Argentine waved from the fireplace. When they were alone, he turned and poured them each another glass of champagne. "To pleasure before business," he said impishly.

She drank with him. Then he took her glass and set it down on the great rock mantle. He took her into his arms, and when they kissed, his powerful body seemed to radiate a current of heat that penetrated her silk gown.

He stepped back and held her at arm's length. "I want to watch you undress before the fireplace. I want to see the golden glow of light touch and caress your hair and body, Jessica. Will you do that for me?"

She nodded and slowly unfastened the long string of pearl buttons of her silk blouse down to her waist. She removed the blouse and then unbuttoned her long skirt and let it slip to the floor. The fire felt warm on her skin, but not as warm as the smoldering heat coming from his dark eyes.

Jessie's figure was so perfect that she had no need of a corset. The only undergarments she was wearing tonight were petticoats and a chemise. When she stepped out of them, she heard his sigh of admiration.

"You are more beautiful than a Greek sculpture," he whispered, coming forward. He placed his fingertips on her lush breasts and she shivered. She bent her head back, and her long, reddish hair was highlighted by the flames. Then Dante bent and kissed her nipples lovingly. Jessie felt her legs tremble with anticipation as he drew her to him again and kissed her passionately. He swept her up and placed her on the long dining room table and undressed himself before the hot fire.

When he stood before her fully unclothed, she saw that he was lean and muscular and very large. He slipped to the table and lay down on top of her, his weight supported by his arms. They kissed again and she pressed her soft, flat belly against his big erection, blanketing it with her own heat. She slid up to lock and roll his throbbing member between her strong thighs. He raised up and she reached down and gripped him, hearing him take a sharp intake of breath.

"Can we roll over without falling off?" she asked.

"This is wider than the Belgian's back and it doesn't move," he said. "I think we can."

They did. Jessie sat up and took his member and began to rub it back and forth across the slick moistness of her center. She closed her eyes and moved him back and forth, a little deeper each time, and when his hips began to thrust upward, she spread her legs wide and drove her hips down onto him, feeling his manhood drive up into her wetness.

He groaned and reached for her. They kissed as she rocked and moved up and down on him. He caressed her breasts and then pulled her down so that he could use his tongue on them. For ten minutes, Jessie rode the Argentinian.

"You're killing me," he finally panted, his breathing coming hard and his hands moving over her body rapidly. "I want you under me now!"

Again they reversed, only now Dante was on top and deep inside of her. Jessie knew that he was nearing the end of his control. She lifted her knees and allowed him to penetrate her fully. She gripped both edges of the heavy dining room table and gave him the freedom to ravage her breasts with his hungry mouth. She gave herself to him fully.

He buried his face between the mounds of her breasts and then his lips moved from one erect, swollen nipple to the other, back and forth, laving them furiously as his hips moved faster and harder at her. He inhaled her woman-scent. The table was rock hard, and each powerful thrust of his hips sent sharp jolts of intense pleasure and pain through her body.

The princess had told her that Dante Manalos was the world's best lover, and he was proving it now as he lifted her ever higher and tortured her deliciously. Jessie had thought to drive him to release first, but now she realized that *she* might be the one to lose control first. She threw her long legs up in the air and locked them around his narrow waist. She used her body like a geisha, playing his thick instrument, until, suddenly, she felt him stiffen. Then his body began to plunge wildly as he released great torrents of his seed deep into her eager body. Jessie also lost control and began to buck wildly, and they were swept away in wave after wave of ecstacy.

Later, Dante pushed himself up weakly on one elbow and stared down at her. "Jessica," he panted, "I have *never* had a woman like you before. I cannot bear to stop this madness until I leave tomorrow."

She held him close. "My dear, brave Argentine *gaucho*," she whispered in his ear, "in order that we might both walk upright tomorrow, can we at least find a bed before you go for another ride?"

Jessica waved goodbye to Dante and closed the door. She was exhausted but well satisfied, and she hoped that Dante would be both safe and successful in their Argentine railroad adventure. She had given him a conditional bill of sale for the crossbred cattle, and gave her foreman instructions to drive the small but very valuable herd down to Galveston Bay, where it would be met by one of her freighters bound for South America.

She came back inside and closed the door to find Ki watching her. Of course, he would know that she and Dante had been lovers; they had few secrets between them, which accounted for their deep friendship. Ki himself often took a woman, one smart enough to see past the fact that he was not all Caucasian. And those women always came back to the samurai for seconds.

"What did you think of him?" she asked.

"He is a good man," Ki said. "The real question is, what did *you* think of him?"

Jessie laughed. "Shame on you, Ki! Come and have some tea with me. Then I think I will take a nap."

"I'm afraid the nap might have to wait," he said.

"What do you mean?"

Ki held the letter out to her. Jessie took it and read the return address. Mrs. Candace Whitman. The letter was postmarked in Alder two weeks ago. "Why did it take so long to get here?" she asked, tearing the envelope open and shaking the letter out before smoothing it on an antique hallway table.

"I don't know," he replied. "The postal service is very poor in this country."

"You can say that again," Jessie groused. Her worst fears were quickly realized as she read about Buzz

Ramsey's true identity, and the killing of the Slade brothers.

Jessie dropped the letter and sighed. "I'm afraid Candace is in serious trouble and young Henry is in an even worse fix." She told the samurai the contents of the letter, and then picked it up to read the last few lines out loud.

"'Buzz made me promise to write and ask for your help, though I would have anyway. He says the Slades promised that their kinfolk and maybe friends would come seeking retribution. I really don't care anymore, Jessie. All that matters to me is that Henry is saved from a life of lawlessness and an early grave. You must remember that he was a *good* boy, a fine boy, who I fear will quickly go bad under the influence of Buzz Ramsey. It is too late for Buzz, but maybe you can save my son.'"

Jessie looked at her samurai. "You were right," she said wearily. "I will have to catch up on my sleep some other time. Please prepare for us to leave at once."

Ki nodded and hurried away. He would have her magnificent stallion, Sun, saddled and ready within a half-hour, along with all the supplies and provisions they'd need. But Alder was only a hundred miles distant. And if they rode hard and met no trouble along the way, they could reach it by tomorrow evening.

Jessie rounded up her foreman, Ed Wright, and told the old cowboss, "Ki and I will have to be gone for a while. I wish I could tell you how long, but I can't."

The tall, graying Texan nodded. He was accustomed to these sudden departures, and no explanation was required or expected. "You know the ranch will take care of itself," he said. "I'll have that Galveston-bound herd heading out by tomorrow. I had sort of planned to prod it along myself."

"I'm sorry," Jessie said. "But you'll be needed here

in my absence. Send Perk along to ride herd and tell him and the boys to ride extra careful. I would not be exaggerating to tell you that those bulls and heifers are mighty valuable to my friend from Argentina."

"Is he going to help you get that railroad contract?"

Jessie nodded. Ed Wright was the only man beside Ki that she confided in about her business. And though the man had only three years of formal education, he had a keen business mind, and had often counseled her father before his death. Had it not been for the old cow-man's intense loyalty to Circle Star, he could have founded his own ranch and been very successful.

"Yes," she told him. "I'm worried about his safety, but he would go on criticizing his president with or without my encouragement. I just hope he can get the order."

"He'd be doing the whole derned country a big favor, going with Starbuck," Ed grunted.

When Jessie simply nodded and turned to leave, the Circle Star foreman said, "You take care and stick close to Ki, Miss Starbuck. I won't sleep sound until you both return."

Jessie walked back, put her arms around his neck, and gave him a big hug. "Since my father died, you and Ki are all the support I have, Ed. Take care of yourself." She kissed him on the cheek and walked away.

Ten minutes later, she and Ki were galloping north-west toward Alder. The letter was two weeks old. What if the Slade family had already come calling on that poor woman?

Jessie tried not to think about it. She gave Sun his head, and the big stallion stretched out his neck and raced like the wind.

Beside her, Ki was thinking along similar lines. But his fears went one layer deeper. What about the boy and the outlaw? Either he or Jessica would have to remain in

Alder and protect Mrs. Whitman, while the other would have to go retrieve Henry. Either way, it would leave Jessica without his services. Leave her vulnerable to attack by enemies.

The samurai found himself torn by worry because he could not be in two places at once. Then he had an idea. They would all go after the boy! That way, they would stand united against every adversity.

He hoped that Jessica saw the wisdom in this. He was not one to suggest things, and, until the very last moment, he would not. But it seemed the only solution. And if it came down to a choice between Jessica and the widow Whitman's life, Ki knew he would save his employer and friend.

But what if it came down to a choice between Henry and Jessica? Ki audibly groaned at the thought and forced himself to avoid that terrible consideration. As always in life, he must be more patient and learn to take what adversities *did* come at him and not attempt to consider those that simply *might* come.

Ki let his paint horse run, knowing that he could not stay even with Jessica Starbuck.

★

Chapter 5

They galloped into Alder, Texas, late the next afternoon, weariness etched deep in the lines of their faces.
Even Sun, practically tireless, now seemed to labor with
each stride. Jessie rounded the corner of Mrs. Whitman's street, then she cried, "Oh my God! Ki, we're too
late!"

The house was gone. In its place was nothing but a
pile of ashes and half-burned rubble. Jessie reined the
stallion in and dismounted. She was heartsick. "Hold
the horses," she whispered. "There is a chance that
Candace might have gotten out alive. I'll ask the neighbors."

She spotted an old woman wrapped in a shawl. The
poor dear's head was nodding as she drowsed, but Jessie
decided she might be the quickest source of information.

"Excuse me!" She entered the old lady's yard and
walked up to her porch. The house was run down, the
windows broken or missing entirely. There were calico
cats running all over the place. Their smell was overpowering.

"Excuse me," Jessica repeated softly, not wishing to

startle the old woman out of her nap. "I need some information."

The old woman's head snapped up and she blinked a few times and worked her lips over toothless gums. "Kin I hep you, pretty lady?" she asked sweetly.

Good, Jessica thought, her mind is working even if her sense of smell is not. "Yes. I am a friend of Mrs. Whitman and her son, Henry. Can you tell me what happened to her?"

"Her house burnt down," the old lady said almost cheerfully. "Right down to the ground."

"I know that. But what happened to *her?*"

"Went away with some men. Saw them. Bad men who set her house on fire." The woman crooked her finger at Jessie. "I don't think that she wanted to go."

Jessie swallowed. At least Candace was alive. "Has the sheriff or anyone gone after her yet?"

"Sheriff Turner is a damned coward!" the old woman said with surprising vehemence. "A cluck, cluck, chicken!"

"Which way did the men go?" The old woman pointed northwest, back into New Mexico. "Thank you," Jessie said, turning to leave.

"You and the Chinaman going to kill them?"

Jessie took a deep breath. "I think we might have to," she said honestly. "How many were there?"

"About twenty." The woman shook her head, sucked her lips into her mouth, and said, "They'll kill *you*. Or make you wish they had."

"No they won't," Jessie vowed softly as she walked away.

They rode their horses into town and tied them up before the sheriff's office. The moment they walked inside, Jessie had a sinking feeling that the old woman had been correct in her assessment of the sheriff. The place was dirty, and the man himself seedy-looking and unkempt. It just stood to reason that someone who exhibited no pride whatsoever in his appearance would have little interest in meeting his obligations.

The sheriff was reading a month-old newspaper. He was only about twenty-five, but he was already forty pounds overweight and going to seed. He even wore old bib overalls. He looked more like a poor dirt farmer than a lawman.

He smiled, laid the newspaper down across his knees, and shifted his round-toed boots on his scarred desktop. "Kin I hep you?" he said, not bothering to get up, but sure eyeing her chest with interest.

"I doubt it," Jessie said, her voice curt and bearing no friendliness. "I'd like to know if you have investigated the abduction of Mrs. Candace Whitman."

The sheriff dragged his feet off his desk and slowly sat up in his chair. "She died in the fire," he said matter-of-factly. "Terrible shame it was."

Ki stepped forward, his arms folded across his chest. "We've heard that she was abducted by a gang of men. Probably the Slade family."

"Who askt you, Chinaman? Woman, you git this—"

Ki moved quickly. Like Jessie, he had seen insolence and sloth the moment he walked into the office. Like Jessie, he had also decided that courtesy and cooperation were not in this man's vocabulary. And now, with this final insult, Ki grabbed the fat man and lifted him right out of the chair. He slapped him once in the face, but hard. Very hard. The sheriff's lips broke and bled and his eyes glazed. Ki eased him back into his swivel chair.

"Now," he said gently, "you will address the lady politely. Her name is Miss Jessica Starbuck and my name is Ki. Tell us everything that you know."

The sheriff verified the old woman's opinion. Instead of reacting with anger or outrage at being slapped like a child, he touched his broken lips, saw the blood, and paled. "You really hurt me bad," he whispered.

"You haven't seen anything yet," Jessie said. "And you're wasting our valuable time."

"All right. All right!" He dragged a dirty handkerchief out of his overalls pocket and held it to his mouth. It muffled his words, but they were understandable.

"I heard that she was taken away, but I didn't believe it."

"Why not?" Jessie shouted.

"Well . . . well, there was no proof. Just that crazy old Nelson woman and a couple others like her or worse."

Jessie wanted to swear a blue streak, but didn't. "The Slades. Do you know where they were from?"

"Maybe Wyoming."

"What makes you say so?" Ki demanded, clearly disappointed that they were from such a distant territory.

"The undertaker found a letter on the body of Josh Slade."

"Do you still have it?"

"No. I throwed it away."

Ki hauled the man out of his chair. "Then you find it."

"But it's in the town garbage pile, out east of town!" the man wailed.

"Mister," Jessie said, her voice hard and unsympathetic. "We've just ridden a hundred miles on the basis of one letter, and we'll ride another thousand if we have to on the basis of another letter. Now you get moving before I tell Ki to pluck out your eyes!"

The fat sheriff glanced up at the impassive samurai and their eyes locked for a moment. Then the sheriff piled out of his chair and headed for the door on the run.

It was almost sundown and the sheriff was up to his knees in garbage—stinking, flyblown garbage. He had alternately begged, pleaded, cried, and pouted but Jessie and Ki had remained indifferent and impassive.

"Here it is!" he cried just as the sun was setting. He pulled his arm out of the garbage and wiped the envelope clean, then held it skyward and whimpered, "Oh thank you, Lord!"

"Open it up and read it out loud," Jessie commanded.

The sheriff obeyed. "'Micah and Josh. Ma died last month of the fever and about fifty goddamn Crow injuns ran off six of our horses and stole your big sister. Get your skinny asses home and we'll go after them. Pa.'"

Jessie glanced at Ki, then back at the sheriff. "Postdated Cheyenne?"

"Yeah, just like I told you."

"Thanks, Sheriff," Jessie said without warmth. She and Ki reined their weary horses around and headed north.

"Hey," the sheriff called, "it's forty miles to the nearest town in that direction!"

Jessie had no intention of pushing either herself or Sun any forty miles. After dark, they would make camp somewhere out in the hills because they were all nearing their physical limits and needed rest. But they'd be up and gone before daylight.

The blizzard struck them fifty miles east of Pueblo, Colorado, and there was no place to hide. The land was almost perfectly flat and there wasn't even a tree in sight. Not that she and Ki had not seen it coming, because they had. But out in eastern Colorado, there were vast distances where you could find nothing to block the wind. Fortunately, they had brought their heavy leather coats, but as the wind howled and the snow flattened to drive almost horizontally into their faces, Jessie knew that they had to find shelter—and fast. She rode in very close to the samurai and yelled into the storm, "We have to find a place to get out of the wind before we freeze to death!"

Ki nodded. He had been thinking the same, and as the visibility had begun to close down on them, he had desperately searched the horizon for any sign of shelter. A stand of trees, a sodhouse, even a buffalo wallow, if it came down to saving themselves and turning the horses loose to walk with the wind.

And finally, just as a wall of wind-driven snow was about to obliterate it, Ki thought that he spotted the square hump of a structure about three miles to the north.

"I think there's a house up ahead!" he shouted.

Jessie could not hear him, but when he pointed into the storm, she knew that he had seen something. The samurai's senses were extraordinary. Hope flared and she lowered her head to the storm and rode on and on, feeling the numbness seeping ever deeper into her body.

To take her mind off the cold, she thought about the men she loved, starting with Longarm, a man who thrilled her with his caresses and charmed her with his easy humor. Longarm was like a wild thing that you wanted to catch and tame. But you knew that, if you did, the best part, the wildness, would die. Jessie thought of Dante Manalos too, and of others she had known. If she and Ki survived this ordeal and were successful in rescuing Candace and Henry, then she thought perhaps she might take a cruise down through the warm Caribbean and on to Argentina. But that would all depend on Dante. Still, the idea of warm air, tropical breezes, and glittering silver sands was so real to her now she wished she could turn Sun around and gallop south until she was warm again.

It seemed like hours before Sun just stopped dead in his tracks. The big stallion shook his head back and forth. Then Ki was on the ground, leading both her and the animals around the corner of a small sod house, the kind which dotted the prairies of Oklahoma, Kansas, and Nebraska, but were less frequently found in Colorado. The effect of leaning forward into the wind and having it suddenly gone was astonishing. Jessie almost pitched forward over her horse's neck. Snow was swirling off the roof of the soddie and whipping around the corners, but the direct force of it was gone.

Ki helped her down and she staggered. Her legs had lost their feeling, and she almost dropped to the frozen earth; would have, if the samurai had not caught her and half dragged, half carried her through an open doorway into the house.

It was deserted, probably only a few months ago by the looks of the interior. Yet it had already been used by many travelers, for their litter and campfire ashes were very evident. Someone had even ripped off the door and used part of it for firewood.

Ki gathered up the unburned portion and then busted it into kindling. He had taken off his gloves and Jessie wondered how he had kept his hands from freezing. Maybe he hadn't. She was so cold she could hardly move, yet move she did. While Ki worked at starting a fire in the small tin barrel that had been converted to a cooking and heating stove, Jessie went outside to get their freezing horses. Sun snorted anxiously, yet he trusted Jessie enough to duck his head and charge through the doorway. Ki's horse followed without hesitation. The two animals half-filled the small one-room house. They snorted nervously at the fire which Ki had managed to get started, but they did not stampede.

Jessie looked up at the ceiling. As in most soddies, whoever had lived there had covered it with cheap muslin in the hope of catching falling dirt. The muslin now billowed with the weight of the dirt which constantly eroded from the sod roof. Jessie reached up and tore the muslin away, and the dirt cascaded to the earthen floor. The muslin was badly soiled and water-stained because these sod houses always leaked during heavy rains. The material was very near rotted, but she thought that anything would be better than an open doorway. So while Ki nursed the precious fire until it began to smoke and spat, Jessie pulled a few hook-nails out of the dirt walls. With the nails and the muslin, she was able to hang a curtain over the doorway.

"There," she said. "It won't keep out the cold, but it should block out the wind and swirling snow."

Ki nodded. His fire was already starting to warm things up a little, and the barrel-stove was snapping and popping as the metal expanded to the heat.

Jessie untied their saddlebags and bed rolls. They soon cooked fresh beef and fried potatoes and washed it down with canteen water. "A little dessert," Jessie said afterward, handing the samurai a big package of cookies that her cook had insisted they take.

The fire was burning hotly now. "We were lucky to find this place," Ki said, "but I sure don't understand how people live surrounded by dirt all year long."

Jessie looked around the little sod house. And though she was grateful for shelter from the blizzard, she could not help but agree with the samurai. "It's like living in a grave," she said. "I think I'd go crazy with the damp earth smell always in my nostrils. I've talked to the wives of many homesteaders, and they always mention the dirt that keeps falling into their cooking food, on their plates, and even in their faces at night. The ceiling cover of muslin helps but it can't stop the centipedes, sow bugs, or earthworms that are constantly burrowing through the walls."

"With so little wood on the prairies, this is about as comfortable a home as they can afford," Ki said. "But if I were a sodbuster, I would always wonder if the roof was going to collapse and bury my wife and children."

Jessie looked at him. "What about yourself?"

"It would not matter. My life is not important."

"It is to me."

The samurai chuckled. "I thought we were theorizing."

"I guess we are," Jessie conceded. "Ki?"

"Yes."

"What do you think will happen when we get to Cheyenne?"

"We'll find the Slade gang and probably kill many of them," he said, staring at the cherry-red stove that was half burnt out, so that you could see specks and cracks of flames. "I'm sure of that much. But I don't know about Mrs. Whitman. She did not seem strong enough to endure a great deal of punishment. She had lost her husband . . . then a man she had pinned her future on, and finally Henry. Mrs. Whitman has had much grief to bear in a short time."

"I think that she is the kind that will grow stronger with adversity, not weaker," Jessie said. "I detected it in her letter."

Ki nodded. "I hope you are right. I am most concerned about Henry. We can find him and take him away from Buzz Ramsey, but if he does not go of his own free will, we have accomplished nothing."

"I agree. He would hate us and his mother, and soon return to ride the outlaw trail with Buzz until he was eventually shot or hanged."

Ki looked at her. "There is one other thing that we have not considered. What if the Slades find Ramsey and the boy before we do? We don't even know where they are headed."

"I know that," Jessie said. "But it seems to me we have no choice but rescue Candace first."

"You are correct," the samurai said as he opened the stove and tossed in more of their precious wood. "At least with her, we have a trail. Good night, Jessica."

The samurai lay down in his blankets and went to sleep. Jessie sat beside the fire for another few minutes and then lay down herself. The firelight made dancing figures on the sod roof. Little pieces of dirt steadily fell on them, the horses, and the floor. Outside the blizzard was howling, and she wondered if it would leave much snow on the ground.

Jessica Starbuck was a woman who enjoyed challenges and measured her ability by the way she was able to overcome adversity. It did not matter whether or not adversity came in the form of a difficult business transaction where her competitors were out to skin her for their own financial gain, or if it were something like overcoming the elements on this trackdown to Cheyenne. In the former case, the stakes were usually to be counted in the millions of dollars to be won or lost. But in this case, the stakes were even higher because two, maybe even three, lives hung in the balance—the boy's, his mother's, and perhaps even Micah and Joshua Slade's sister, captured by Crow Indians.

And if Jessica Starbuck had not missed her sleep for two nights running, she might have stayed awake again just thinking about it. But instead she pulled a horse blanket over her body and a Stetson over her face to keep off the falling dirt.

And she slept until dawn, to awaken to an ocean of snow and the cold, cobalt-blue skies of eastern Colorado.

★

Chapter 6

Candace Whitman also felt like she was living in a grave, only hers was a small, chill root cellar eighty miles north of Cheyenne, Wyoming.

The Slade family ranch was located on the north fork of the Platte River, and it was impressive in terms of both acreage and number of cattle. But Candace didn't know or care about that. As she lay in a pile of buffalo robes and listened to both the howling wind and the muffled but never ending arguments of the Slade family as to her fate, all she could think about was her abduction and the long ride north.

The Slades had come in the night, faceless riders who had crashed into her home and pulled her out of bed and hurled her to the floor to cower in the blinding light of their torches.

"Where is he?" they had demanded. "Where is Buzz Ramsey, the one who killed Micah and Josh?"

"I don't know. I swear I don't know."

"He has your boy!"

"I still don't know. Please, what are you doing with that torch? Oh, no! Please!"

They had demanded over and over to know the

whereabouts of Buzz Ramsey. And when she could tell them nothing, they had gagged and bound her and thrown her across a horse. Candace vaguely remembered crying out for them to spare her mother. But as she was being taken away, she had seen the flames licking up to the sky, and she knew that her mother had died in that house. It was a frame house, and it would burn so hot that they might not even find the ashes of her frail bones. Thank heavens the poor old woman had been near the end of her life. Her body had been wasting away with some terrible inner affliction. Candace prayed the old woman had died in her sleep, poisoned by the smoke.

Candace had been taken north, and only after days on horseback had she realized that her real nightmare was yet to begin; somewhere in Colorado, they had hit upon the idea of trading her to the Crow Indians for one of their own, a woman named Maud Slade.

When she had first heard Jeb Slade's proposal, Candace had tried to fight down an overwhelming sense of panic. She had often heard gruesome stories about the fate of white women traded to the renegade Indians, who still refused to be yoked to the peace treaties and the reservations. She had heard that the Indians used the white women as prostitutes, and that they were routinely beaten, scratched, spat upon, and vilified by the squaws. True, those stories had mostly dealt with women taken by Comancheros and traded to the horrible Apache, but Indians were all the same, weren't they? They were heathens, and they would use her like an animal.

Candace had stopped eating, for she preferred to die rather than be traded to the Indians. But when the Slades realized her plan, they had threatened to kill Henry when they found Buzz Ramsey. Threatened not only to kill him, but torture him to death.

Candace had begun to eat again.

But now she sensed that a decision had been made to ride north to find the Crow and make a trade. They were to leave when the storm died. Candace stared into the darkness and wondered if she would lose her mind when the first Crow brave raped her. She almost hoped she would.

She slept again, but when the door of the root cellar was jerked open, she was hauled outside and across the wind-blown snow to the ranch headquarters. The sudden warmth of the huge fireplace struck her forcibly and her knees buckled. She did not fight as they lifted her up and carried her into the dining room.

"Here's meat, potatoes, and tinned peaches," the patriarch of the family growled. His name was Napoleon, and he was big and loud, a man in his sixties with mean eyes and a sabre scar across one cheek. "Crows like fat women better than skinny ones. That's why they took Maud. She's hog-fat."

"I'm not hungry."

"Eat, damn you!" The man grabbed her hair and bent her head back. "We got word that Buzz Ramsey and your boy robbed a stagecoach in Utah Territory and a bank in eastern Nevada. Killed a driver and a bank manager."

Candace tried to shake her head. "I don't believe my boy had any part of it!" she spat.

Napoleon glared into her eyes. "I wish I could hear you scream when the first buck Indian climbs on you, woman."

Candace swallowed. "If you don't keep your part of our bargain, you will certainly rot in hell, sir."

The man snarled and released her hair. "All right, I'll keep mine. We get your boy away and set him free after we kill Ramsey; in return, you eat and get fat for the Crow."

He picked up a spoon. "Eat, Mrs. Whitman. You may not get as good as a dog when you become a Crow's woman."

She looked around at the grinning faces. She was the only woman among them, and she could see lust in their eyes, though none had dared assault her yet. Seeing the cruelty in their faces, Candace could not help but feel a deep sense of pity for Buzz Ramsey. He might be an outlaw, a bank robber, and highwayman, but he was not an animal, not like these men.

Napoleon Slade stomped over to peer out the window. "The storm is passing and I see blue sky off to the north. We leave first thing tomorrow morning. With any luck, we'll catch that band of Crow up near the Yellowstone River and have Maud back here with us this time next week."

"I'd rather have Mrs. Whitman," one of them said. "She's prettier."

"Shut up, Ezra! Maud was your sister."

"She was still big and mean," Ezra said. "And she hated all men."

Candace looked up at him. "I don't suffer from that hatred," she said. "But even if I did, it wouldn't matter, because none of you qualify."

It took a moment for the Slades to realize they had been insulted, but when they did understand, instead of getting angry, they all started laughing. All except Ezra, whose narrow face flushed red, and whose eyelids slitted like those of a cat watching a battered, soon-to-be-eaten mouse.

"When we ride into Crow country and find us that band of renegades that took Maud, you'll see who's a man and who ain't. And you may not think much of us now, but if shootin' and scalpin' starts, by Gawd, I'll bet you'll be screaming for the Slade family to win."

Candace guessed that Ezra was probably right, but did it really matter? If there was trouble and the Slades were killed, wouldn't that at least save Henry and Buzz?

Two weeks later, when they rode into the Bighorn Basin of northeastern Wyoming, Candace was still pondering that very same question. What if she grabbed a gun and shot one of the Crow warriors and started a gunfight? Even if she were slain, at least that would be the end of the Slades. She decided that would be her course of action. To be traded away to the Indians for an empty promise that mercy be given her son was a bad bargain. If the Slades caught Buzz Ramsey, they would surely kill both him and her dear Henry.

Candace no longer expected to live. She surveyed the rugged, untamed Montana country and felt the presence of death all around her. At night, when she had to hunt wood for the cooking fire, she often found arrowheads and the bones of animals. This country silently screamed of great Indian battles and thundering buffalo hunts. They said that, to the west, there were towering gushers of hot, smelly water and boiling pools. Candace did not believe that, for it was much too cold up here in these dark, frightening forests.

The rivers were choked with ice; snow lay deep in the shadowed gulleys and yawning canyons, waiting for more to fall. The aspen shivered in the crackling air. They were always cold, always alert, with their rifles up and ready.

Old Napoleon Slade was particularly vocal about the bone-numbing weather, the long miles he rode in the saddle, the Crows that he hated for stealing his only daughter, the lack of good red meat due to the unexpected scarcity of wild game. Candace turned a deaf ear to his curses. If anything, the old man's acute discomfort gave her strength, for it meant that these men were vulnerable too. There were twenty-three of them, and they were all interrelated. She knew most by name, but others were just lean, ugly men with bearded faces and cold eyes. They looked tough and they all carried the new repeating Winchesters while they expected the Crow to have bows and arrows or at best, ancient, single-shot percussion models. To a man, the Slades bragged that a white man with a Winchester repeater was worth ten redskins armed with their traditional weapons.

"Listen!" Ezra said, one morning as they mounted up in a fresh snowfall. "Do you hear it?"

"Wolves?"

Old Napoleon nodded. He pulled his thick sheep-skin-lined coat up around his jowels and said, "It's wolves, and they're chasin' somethin' down in the next valley. Could be we can get some fresh meat without firing a shot and bringing on the Crow by surprise."

"Let's go, then!" Ezra cried.

Candace rode with both hands clenched on the saddlehorn. Her horse wore a halter instead of a bridle, and a lead rope led to one of the riders. Now, her horse was pulled along in a wild stampede as the Slades burst out of the camp and raced toward the next valley.

Candace had to struggle just to stay in the saddle. Her horse was the oldest and slowest of the lot—a measure that ensured she would not try to run away. The horse was also a stumbler, and she feared that it would trip and fall. They raced headlong through brush, across bright patches of snow, over icy creeks, through boggy fields of frozen pine needles, and then across a wide, high ridge.

"Looka there!" Napoleon cried, reining his horse to a halt. "Elk!"

Candace stared in fixed horror. There were two bull elk, standing facing in opposite directions to protect each other's flanks. One glance told the entire story. The elk were blocking a narrow defile of rock and ensuring the retreat of their herd. It was a gallant stand, for the wolves were thick and desperate with hunger.

"Hold up!" Napoleon said when one of his men levered a fresh shell into his rifle. "Let's wait until the wolves hamstring 'em. Then we'll ride on down and chase them off and take the meat."

"They might not chase off," a man said. "There must be fifty wolves in that bunch, and they're all winter-starved."

"If they don't chase," Napoleon said, "*then* we'll have to shoot the bastards. But let's see if we can do this quiet. I'd rather find the Crow than have them find us."

"How come?" a cousin named Jubal asked. "You changed your mind about tradin' with old Buffalo Horse?"

Napoleon nodded. "If we could catch them by surprise, it might be easier just to kill 'em all off."

"But what about Maud? You know that she'd be the first one that'd die!"

"I didn't say it'd be easy. Look at them two big sons-abitches fight!"

Candace watched, feeling sick to her stomach. A huge gray wolf had managed to get his teeth into the throat of one of the bulls. The elk was slinging its head about and the wolf was being snapped back and forth, but it hung on with its powerful jaws. Blood was pouring out of the elk's throat and it was bellowing and thrashing, covering the thin snow with bright, crimson drops. It folded to its knees and the pack swarmed over it. The wolves seemed to go into a killing frenzy, while the second elk, without its rear quarters protected, was soon whirling around and around trying to keep the wolves off its back legs. It was kicking, slashing with its huge horns, impaling wolves and tossing them high into the air, only to have others throw themselves at its head. It was about to die.

Candace could not stand the sight. While the men were all staring at the terrible scene of death below, she reached out and grabbed a sixgun.

"Hey!" its owner yelled.

Candace emptied the gun into the air. The wolves stopped and turned; even the bull elk froze for an instant.

"Goddamn you!" Napoleon yelled. "You let her get your gun. If there's any Injuns within fifteen miles, they've heard those shots!"

The man whose gun Candace had taken reared back and slapped her so hard she was knocked from her horse and landed on the frozen ground. The Slades took her horse and left her prostrate, knowing she had nowhere to run. Then they took off after the wolves. Candace crawled back to her feet. She stood up in time to see the second elk whirl in the face of the men and horses. It trumpeted and disappeared through the slice of rock, racing after its herd.

"Run," she screamed to herself as well as the surviving bull. "Run!"

The wolves were on the fallen elk, ripping and tearing. Carried away in a blood frenzy, they would not leave their fresh kill. When the Slades burst into their pack, they spun around and stood their ground, crazed by the taste of meat.

The wolves died in a hail of gunfire. The Slades proved themselves expert riflemen and they did not waste their lead. In a moment, the ground was littered with dead and dying wolves; those that broke and ran were shot down before they could reach the cover of trees.

When the thunder of rifle-fire rolled across the great Big Horn basin and finally died, Candace was in the forest and running for her own life.

There was no snow under the heavy lid of the forest. It was dim and very cold and Candace ran without thought or direction. Escape!—that was all that she wanted. Better even to die of exposure to the cold or of starvation than be traded to the Indians. Her act to save the bull elk had been unthinking, totally instinctive.

How long would it be until the Slades turned back to the ridge and saw that she was missing? Five minutes? Perhaps a half-hour? Candace raced down a mountainside, her arms windmilling wildly, her legs pumping so fast that she was completely out of control. She hit a small frozen stream and her feet went out from under her. She stifled a cry and went tumbling downward, striking rocks and tearing through a large stand of manzanita. Somehow, she retained consciousness and rolled to her feet. Dazed, she staggered on until she came to the base of the mountain and found a stream. She followed it, trying to stay on the rocks so that she would leave no tracks.

Hours passed. She was exhausted, torn by brush, and struggling to move. She had heard the Slades coming after her, heard their furious shouts. She knew that twenty-three hard men were fanning out across this mountainside. Suddenly, Candace burst out of the forest and before her lay a valley and a big Indian village. She saw squaws and children racing about frantically. They were throwing dirt out of their tipis, and that confused Candace. She turned to race back into the forest.

A band of at least eight fierce-looking Indians emerged from the trees to close off her path of escape. They carried lances, war clubs, bows, and arrows. Their leader, a tall, powerfully built chief wearing buffalo horns, raised his bow and arrow and pointed it at her heart. He looked deep into her eyes and shook his head as if to tell her something. Candace had been about to scream, but the chief's eyes made her change her mind. She clamped her mouth shut and raised her chin.

The chief lowered his bow, and a warrior leaped forward. He grabbed her cheeks and dug his thumb and forefinger into them. When her mouth flew open, a piece of soft leather was pushed halfway down her throat. Candace gagged and was roughly pushed ahead toward the Indian camp. An old squaw grabbed her hand, shoved her into a tipi, and she landed in a shallow grave. The squaw tied her hands behind her back and bound her ankles together. She was not blindfolded, however; and beside her on the floor of the tipi lay the village's young women and children, all in similar graves. Candace listened to the sharp cries of the old squaws outside. She waited, her body pressed to the cold earth, her heart beating so loudly that she could feel it striking at her compressed rib cage. *Why,* she raged, *didn't I scream and let him put an arrow into me? Why didn't I make him kill me?*

Long minutes passed. She smelled cooking meat and heard a squaw laugh. Another joined in. *What is going on?* Candace thought. *Don't they even know that the Slades are coming and—*

Her eyes widened with understanding. This village was bait for a trap! Of course it was. These shallow graves were—

A volley of Winchester rifles cut through the village like a scythe through wheat. Bullets tore through the tipis as if they were made of paper. Probing lead crisscrossed through the tipis so thickly that nothing above ground level was left unscathed.

Candace heard children and babies screaming. She raised her head a fraction and felt a bullet whistle past her ear. The rifle fire seemed to last an eternity but, when it stopped, a deadly silence fell over the Indian village. The barking dogs had been forever silenced, and maybe the old squaws as well.

Candace heard the unmistakable voice of Napoleon Slade when he yelled. "They *got* to be all dead. Let's go take some scalps, boys!"

She heard the approaching hoofbeats and then, quite suddenly, the cry of a dying white man. Indian screams filled the air as the war party swept out of the forest and caught the Slades from behind, and out of ammunition. Bowstrings hummed, and the soft whirring of feathered arrows ended with a thud as arrowheads struck down the Slades.

Candace heard the sounds of death—a few scattered shots and then more screams and racing hoofbeats.

The squaws drew knives and rushed outside, howling with vengeance, leaving Candace alone with their small children. She stared at their round, curious faces as they all listened to the Crow take Slade scalps.

★

Chapter 7

Jessie and Ki walked into the sheriff's office and introduced themselves.

Sheriff John Walton was in his late twenties, smug, suspicious, and a bit of a dandy. "So," he said, after Jessie had explained their business, "you think that the Slades kidnapped a widow woman named Candace Whitman and brought her up to Wyoming."

"That's right," Jessie answered. "And we're going to bring her back. I always like to check in with the law first, but with your help—or without it—we intend to find Candace and see that the Slades are brought to trial for kidnapping, and the murder of her mother."

"I doubt you'll have any luck at all," Walton said. "You see, Maud Slater was captured by the Crow. Now I sure can't, for the life of me, understand why they'd want her, but maybe they got carried away with their good fortune when they stampeded off the Slade horses. Anyway, they took that big old sow with her warts and mean disposition. It'd be my guess that the Slades needed someone to trade. Is the widow Whitman ugly?"

Jessie flared. "Of course not! But what has that got to

do with anything? She was kidnapped by force, and that is a hanging offense down in Texas."

"Is here too, ma'am. I was just hoping she was ugly; then maybe the Crow wouldn't trade for her. But she'd have to go a ways to be uglier than Maud Slade."

Ki was disgusted with the entire conversation. He said, "Why don't you just tell us how to get to the Slade place, so we can take care of this ourselves?"

"Well," the sheriff said, "you just ride eighty miles north—you can't miss it. The Slade ranch is over a thousand acres. But you want a little piece of advice?"

"No," Jessie said, heading for the doorway.

The sheriff followed them outside and watched them mount their horses. "You've been riding long and hard, I see."

"What's your advice?" Jessie asked bluntly.

"You're a rich woman, Miss Starbuck. Why don't you offer to buy the widow back from the Slades? That is, if they haven't traded her to the Crow Indians yet."

"Uh-uh," Jessie said. "And do you want a little advice?"

"It's a free country, ma'am. Sure, from someone as pretty and rich as yourself, I'll take a piece of advice, for whatever it's worth."

"Get out of the lawman's business, Mr. Walton. If you had any sand, you'd have cleaned out the likes of the Slades when you took office."

The young man's face colored with embarrassment and anger. "That would be a very *fatal* piece of advice and it ain't worth spit, Miss Starbuck. Napoleon Slade owns this county."

Jessie shook her head. "And the law, too, if you're an example."

"Get the hell out of my town," Walton growled.

"Not until morning. Our horses are played out."

"All right, you can stay the night, but don't let me see you tomorrow."

Jessie did not like being threatened and she knew that Ki felt the same way. But they had enough trouble right now, and Candace needed them very badly. So Jessie bit her lip and rode away, hot with anger. You did not sleep with dogs, or you'd get fleas. You did not believe dishonorable men or you were tricked by their lies. Using the few remaining hours of daylight, they stocked up on some provisions and paid the liveryman well to grain and rub down their horses. The long trail had worn both their horses' shoes down to practically nothing, but they managed to get a blacksmith to drop his other work and shoe both animals. Jessie hated to lose the time in Cheyenne, but you could push horses just so hard, even outstanding ones like they both rode. For no matter how big their heart or desire, they would break down and be ruined if pressed beyond their physical limits.

In the morning they saddled up, and as they prepared to take up the trail again, Ki said, "Let's take a little detour back up Main Street."

"Why?" It was a block out of their way, and though it would take only a few minutes, Jessie was curious.

"I want to ask Sheriff Walton about something."

Jessie studied the samurai. She had never questioned him before, and she would not do it now. So they rode back down Main Street, past City Hall and the schoolhouse, the general store, and gunsmith's shop.

Ki dismounted and handed his reins up to Jessie. "This will only take a minute," he said as he walked into the sheriff's office.

A kid no more than fifteen years old was sitting behind Sheriff Walton's office desk, smoking a cigar with his feet up on the desk. When the door opened he almost tipped his chair over backward trying to get his feet down and the cigar out of sight. But when he saw Ki with his long black hair, almond-shaped eyes, and oriental features, he put the cigar back up in his mouth and his expression revealed irritation.

"What do you want?" he demanded.

Ki looked at the boy. "Where is the sheriff?"

"What do you want to know for?"

Ki walked around the desk and grabbed the kid by the shirtfront and threw him over backwards. Boy and swivel chair crashed, and the boy skidded across the floor. When he hit the wall, he sat up fast, slapping his cigar and burning ashes from his clothes.

"Now," Ki said patiently as he walked over and ground the cigar out under his heel before it burned the office down, "please tell me where the sheriff has gone."

All the insolence went right out of the young man. "He rode north to see Napoleon Slade. Who in blazes are you?"

Ki didn't bother to answer. He went out and remounted his horse. "The sheriff is on the Slade payroll, and he's gone ahead to warn them we're coming."

"Damn!" Jessie whispered. "I should have known better than to take the chance."

Ki didn't say a word, but he agreed. The old woman in Alder, Texas, had said that there were twenty Slade riders who had kidnapped Candace Whitman and burned her house down. Those were pretty tough odds against just Jessie and himself. Now their biggest advantage—that of surprise—was gone.

"I think we should pay our visit well after dark," he said as they galloped out of Cheyenne.

"We'll have to," Jessie said. "It'll take that long just to get there."

It was long after dark when they approached the headquarters of the Slade ranch. The lights in the ranch house were burning. The temperature had dropped well below freezing.

Ki and Jessie dismounted and slapped their hands

against their legs in an effort to get the circulation flowing.

"Looks like they're up and waiting to give us a reception," Jessie said.

"Well then, let's not disappoint them. How shall we handle it?"

Jessie studied the layout. The house was what was commonly called a Texas style, one popular on cattle ranches from the Gulf of Mexico all the way to Canada. It had two identical wings with a dogtrot or breezeway in the middle, which folks liked to sit under in the summertime. In this case, the west wing was the one with the fireplace and the living room—probably the kitchen and dining room as well. The east wing would probably have a library as well as the bedrooms.

Around the ranchyard in a loose but complete circle was arranged a bunkhouse, a livery, a blacksmith shop, tack room, smokehouse, barn, and corrals.

"I think we'll have to make them come outside," Jessie said. "Besides, it's too damned cold for my blood up here. Let's warm things up a little."

"You mean with a little fire?"

"How else?" Jessie carried matches, and now she gave several to her samurai. "You start with the barn. I would imagine it might be filled with winter hay and burn very nicely. I'll start at the other edge of the circle and see how the cookshack burns."

Ki smiled. This was what he most liked about working with Jessica Starbuck. When she went to war, she went to war for keeps. Being a rancher herself, she knew with dead certainty that the Slades could not afford to lose an entire barnful of winter hay. Not in this country.

They would have to come out and, when they did, they would be distracted and concerned with the blaze and have to run into the center of the yard. Heat and smoke would blind them and they could be either shot or made to surrender. It was a good plan.

Jessie remounted and galloped around behind the cookshack. She dismounted and drew her sixgun. Tying Sun back in the safety of darkness, she advanced quickly, scooping up handfuls of dead grass and twigs, which she placed at the base of the cook's woodpile. She knelt, removed her gloves, lit a match, and cupped it from the cold breeze. Then she touched it to the grass and twigs, which flamed immediately. The woodpile was dry at the base, and the fire burned greedily as it ate into the bark. After a few moments, Jessie picked up a burning firebrand and hurled it right through the cook-shack window.

Almost immediately, the structure caught on fire, and when Jessie raced on towards the next building, the windows of the cookshack began to fill with a bright orangish glow.

But it was the barn that really went up in flame. One minute it was just a huge, dark silhouette against the star-studded sky; the next it was an inferno as the dried field-hay exploded under its roof.

Jessie raced ahead to the livery barn and then dived behind a water trough. She laid her sixgun across the rim of the trough and waited. She would give them about five minutes. Then, if they did not come out, she would torch the blacksmith shop while Ki would set to burning the tack room. Without harness, saddles, bridles, and blankets, the Slade ranch cowboys would be in serious trouble.

The front door of the ranch house blew open and two old men and an even older woman came hobbling out with their hands over their heads. They were screaming, but Jessie could not hear their voices because of the roar of the barn's hay fire.

Jessie did not understand. Where were the twenty fighting men? Or even the sheriff? She frowned and saw the shadow of the samurai detach from behind the buildings and spring towards the back of the house. Ki was going in the back door just to make sure this was no trap.

She stepped out from the shadows and approached the three old people with caution.

"Where is Candace Whitman?" she demanded.

"Under an Indian and wishing she was in hell!" the old woman screamed.

Suddenly she dropped to the ground, and the old men did the same. Jessie whirled back toward the house and saw Sheriff Walton raise his rifle. She snapped off a shot. It must have been a lucky one, because the lawman threw himself sideways on the porch and fired.

Jessie started running for cover. Her sixgun was no match for a rifle at any distance. The rifle probed for her as she raced back towards the safety of the water trough.

"Sheriff!" Walton turned to see the samurai. "Drop your rifle!"

Sheriff John Walton swung his weapon around and started to pull the trigger, knowing he could not miss this time. But he noticed the samurai's arm flick forward like a spring. And in the brilliant light of the great fire outdoors, he observed a spinning object. His mouth opened and distended as he felt a searing pain that lasted less than an instant before he died with a *shuriken* star-blade in his forehead.

Ki moved over to the man. He removed his *shuriken* blade and wiped it clean on the sheriff's sleeve. He had not wanted to kill the man, for he could have given them answers.

Ki headed across the yard to the three old people. They were like a trio of cobras now that their trick had failed, and they were fighting mad. The men were armed. But as they tried to pull their guns, Ki hit the first one with a knife-hand blow to the neck, which he could have broken had he wished. The old man collapsed like a sack of grain, and his gun spilled into the dirt.

The second man actually did get his weapon out of his waistband, but Ki sent it spinning with a *tegatana* blow. The man howled in pain, and Ki brought the old devil crashing down with a weeping lotus kick behind the knees. Seeing her companions dispatched so roughly caused the old woman to back off in a hurry.

"I ain't armed," she hissed. "You keep your damn hands and feet to yourself, Chinaman!"

"Where is the rest of the family?"

The old woman's chin quivered with hatred and defiance until Ki raised the hard edge of his right hand and bluffed her into thinking he would strike her down.

"All right! They went north into the Crow lands to kill them thievin' Injuns and bring Maud back. And I hope you and that woman are fool enough to go after them."

"We'll go," Jessie vowed, though she was disappointed that the showdown could not have taken place right here in this ranchyard, and that Candace was still out of their reach.

Jessie looked at the two old men, who were trying to pick themselves off the ground. They were both spitting and hissing like a couple of doused tomcats. "Who are they?"

"My two younger brothers. They may not look like much right this minute, but they is both mean as could be!"

"I'll bet." Jessie turned to Ki. "I think we ought to keep riding."

"I agree," Ki said, wasting no time in hurrying towards his horse.

"What about our hay?" the old woman screeched. "We need it for our ranch horses and the milk cow!"

84

Jessie just shrugged. "I guess you'll have to buy some more."

"Goddamn it, Napoleon'll skin you both with a dull knife if the Crow don't first!"

Jessie remounted. The old woman was yelling when she and Ki reined north and touched spurs to gallop into the freezing night. Jessie pulled her collar up to her eyes, but still they bled tears from the cold. She thought about how, only last summer, this entire ordeal had been set in motion on that damned stagecoach from Santa Fe, New Mexico. Had it not been for that blistering hot journey and the fateful meeting between Buzz Ramsey and poor Candace, none of this would have taken place.

It's all Ramsey's fault, she thought. *And he better not have gotten that boy killed yet!*

★

Chapter 8

Buzz Ramsey and Henry Whitman rode into the Nevada boomtown of Jumbo with three dollars between them. They were gaunt, and their mounts were little more than horsehide and bone.

There had been a gold and silver strike in Jumbo, which lay just ahead; a strike that had sent miners and speculators pouring into central Nevada by the thousands. Now, only six months after the strike, Buzz could see that Jumbo offered the standard fare of all mining towns—unlimited action for a man with his talents, but also lots of risks. The mines were operating full shifts, and men were descending into the deep shafts and being raised out of them three times a day. That was how a gambling man could tell if a town was prospecting—the mines never closed, and neither did the saloons, gambling halls, and the house of prostitution. As soon as one shift of miners had spent their pay, another shift was coming off work to take their places.

A gambler couldn't ask for a better place to work. Not even on the old Mississippi River steamboats. No sir! In a place like Jumbo, the gold ran as freely as a

Rocky Mountain river, and the action would not stop until the mines ran out of paydirt.

As they rested their horses for the long grade up to Jumbo, Buzz resolved not to rob any more banks or stagecoaches. For one thing, Henry Whitman absolutely refused to have any part of it, which was understandable. The young man had been raised strict, and with some sense of morals. Buzz sort of liked to think that, if he resisted corrupting Henry, it would be his earthly penance. That way, if there was a God and a day of reckoning, at least he could point out that he had kept Henry from riding the outlaw trail or killing anyone.

Jumbo was backdropped by a tall, round-shouldered mountain about two thousand feet high. It was on the eastern slope of this barren, ugly mountainside that gold and silver had been discovered. The thing that amazed Buzz the most was how anyone in his right mind would ever choose such a desolate place to sink a shaft in hopes of striking it rich.

But they had, and if you rode anywhere in the Nevada deserts or hills, you would witness thousands of those pathetic little mounds of dirt, each a monument to some lonely dreamer who had invested days, weeks, perhaps even months of his life and fortune by digging into some worthless mountainside. Yet even Buzz had to admit that every now and then—just often enough to keep the fools het up with gold fever—some poor devil with nothing but a pick, shovel, and maybe a burro, struck it rich.

It was funny, though; of all the gold strikes that Buzz had ever heard of, not once had the men that made the discovery really profited from it. That was as true with the Forty-niner strike over in California as it was with the fabulous Comstock Lode on Sun Mountain. Nope, the real money was always made by the men who came in afterward—the ones who speculated in wildly soaring real estate and mining stocks. Those who bought

and sold with the cunning and courage of wolverines—
they were the ones that got rich, not the miners.

"What do you think?" he asked the young man beside him.

Henry Whitman had little to say. "It just looks like
most all the others we've passed through. Maybe even a
little bigger than Centipede."

"Hell!" Buzz spat. "Centipede couldn't have com-
pared to Jumbo. There were only sixteen saloons in the
whole damn town. I can count almost twenty just on
one side of the street!"

Henry looked directly into the man's eyes. "You
aren't fixin' to rob the bank this time, are you, Buzz?
You know I won't be a part of it."

Buzz feigned surprise that such a question could even
be considered. "I gave you my word there'd be no more
banks or stagecoaches, didn't I?"

"Yeah, but—"

"Listen, Henry, that last one in Utah was just too
damned inviting. Those Mormons aren't used to men
coming through their towns and having enough courage
to relieve them of their money."

"That may be true," Henry said, "but it's just as true
that, if we hadn't had some damned good horseflesh
between our legs, those Mormons would surely have
relieved us of our lives!"

"They chased us for eighty miles and I only got a
hundred and fourteen dollars!" Buzz complained.
"Those Mormons are so tight-fisted they don't even
trust their own banks. They must keep their money buried under their floors or something."

"Stealing is stealing," Henry said with anger still in
his voice, and the memory of how scared he had been
riding for his life across the Utah desert. "You didn't
even tell me what you were up to, though I should have
guessed."

"No banks this time," Buzz promised. He clapped

the young man on the shoulder and touched his spurs to his horse.

The boy followed and Buzz smiled to himself. He liked young Henry a lot. And in just the short time they had been riding the frontier together, Henry had changed from a boy to a man. He had grown broadshouldered and taller than Buzz, though it would take a few more years for him to fill out to his proper weight and reach his full strength.

They rode into Jumbo and tied their horses in front of a saloon. "Want a drink?" Buzz asked.

"Nope. I want some money to eat with and to buy our poor horses some feed. They're so skinny I'm ashamed to ride them."

"It wasn't my fault them Mormons ran us into the desert," Buzz said. "And the three dollars I have left is seed money for a poker game. I can't even meet the ante without at least that much. But within an hour, you come back into this saloon and find me at the poker table and I'll give you a whole pocketful of gold."

Henry frowned, but knew it was entirely possible. When Buzz was running with luck and not drinking too hard, he was unbeatable. Henry had seen him win a thousand dollars one evening in the space of two hours —more money than most miners earned in a solid year of backbreaking labor.

"All right," Henry said. "I'll mosey around town and come back in an hour."

Buzz said nothing. He wrapped his reins around the hitch rail, his eyes fixed on the door of the saloon that advertised poker tables in the back, no limit. Henry had learned to read a certain kind of expression on his companion's face. It was a look of intense anticipation, which only possessed the man when he came in sight of a poker table. Buzz talked about gold fever; well, he had gambling fever. He lived and breathed cards, and even when they were out on the trail, camped beside a fire, Buzz wanted to play poker. So they played, and, as of now, Henry owed the man a little more than two million dollars. But he was doing better. He never lost more than twenty thousand at a sitting anymore.

When Henry went to bed, Buzz sat up and practiced little tricks that were indispensible to a professional gambler—dealing off the bottom of the deck, pulling a card out of his sleeve, reading marked cards, double dealing. "You have to know how to cheat to catch your opponent cheating," Buzz would say.

But Henry thought that maybe his friend sometimes cheated first. That was why he wanted no part of hanging around a game when Buzz was playing. Because if Buzz got caught cheating, there would be a gunfight, and if you were associated with a card cheat, it was assumed you were part of the action, and guilty too.

Henry liked to listen to the miners. Many of them were from Scotland, England, Wales, and other parts of the world where deep mining was commonplace. They came because they were good at working underground, and most of them became foremen and supervisors of the shifts. But there were also lots of everyday Americans like himself, men who arrived in Nevada from greener pastures, hoping to strike it big and return to wherever it was they had originated.

Henry had noticed right away that, if you listened to the talk, it was never of today but always of tomorrow. Tomorrow, when they would strike it rich. Tomorrow, when they would go home and everyone would call them "Sir!" And tomorrow, when they would marry a proper girl and have a proper home. Wear a coat and tie, belong to a gentlemen's club and smoke fine cigars and sip brandy imported from France. But until then, it was rotgut and whores, lost money at roulette and cards, then back down into the dangerous underground caverns, where foul air and cave-ins killed the dreams of tomorrow with alarming frequency.

"Hey, mate!" a slightly inebriated Englishman said as he blocked Henry's path along the broadwalk. "How about a shell game for two bits?"

Henry shook his head. "Sorry."

"What's the matter, mate? No stomach for a little sport? Or has your mother cut off your allowance? All right, for a lousy nickel, then."

The man and several others within hearing distance laughed outright. Henry flushed with shame and tried to move past the burly Englishman, but the man caught his sleeve and yanked him down.

"Watch the shells, mate," he ordered. "See how I place the pea under this shell?"

His thick, dirty hands moved back and forth over the three small shells and then, with a flourish, they pulled away. "All right, mate, for a bloody nickel, where is the pea? It's easy."

"I haven't got a nickel," Henry said with embarrassment.

"You . . . you don't even have a bloody nickel!" the man shouted, feigning shock and horror. "How bloody pathetic can things be?"

More laughter burned Henry's ears. He started to push past, but the Englishman caught him again. "Then can you tell me for a bloody penny—which shell has the pea?"

A small crowd had gathered and were enjoying the Englishman's sport. Henry knew that he could either submit and be shamed half to death—or he could fight. There was no way he could be diplomatic. Things had already gone much too far. Besides, he knew about the shell game because Buzz had demonstrated how the trick usually worked. The pea was really up the Englishman's sleeve. He would only replace it under one of the shells that Henry failed to choose.

"Well, come on, man! For one bloody cent I can't waste all day on you. It'd take me three days to win enough to buy a bloody ale at a penny a game. Come on bloke, choose!"

Henry straightened up. He stepped forward and, before the Englishman knew what was happening, stomped his boot down on top of the shells, smashing all three to bits. "I guess the little pea wasn't under any of them, was it?" he asked innocently.

The Englishman, half bent over, stared down at the squashed hulls with shock and disbelief. Then, before he could react in rage and take a swing, Henry whipped his best punch up and caught the man squarely under the jaw. The con artist crashed over a hitching rail and landed in the street.

Henry wanted to run. The Englishman was forty pounds heavier and probably a hundred fights more experienced. But Henry knew that he couldn't run.

In the first place, there was his own pride at stake, and in the second, there were now at least fifty men all around who would block his escape. So he took a deep breath and charged the Englishman, hoping to knock him back down and keep him down.

But the man jammed him in the side of the knee with his bootheel, and Henry cried out in pain, feeling as if his leg were broken. He fell, and the Englishman landed on his chest like an enraged animal. The man sledgehammered two thundering punches down into Henry's face. A third would have finished the fight, but Henry whipped up his long legs and hooked his heels into the heavier man's face, then yanked him over backward.

If the Englishman had all the advantages of strength, heft, and experience, Henry at least had the advantage of speed. He was on his feet first, harboring no sense of honor about waiting until his opponent was prepared to defend himself.

He punched the Englishman in the eye and knocked him off his knees. Then he jumped on him and pounded him twice in the face before the Englishman tore him off his chest and rolled up on top of him. At that point, the fight was as good as lost. Henry tried to hook the man with his legs again, but the Englishman was ready now and bent too far forward. He sledged three solid blows to Henry's face, and it was lights out.

Henry awoke on an examining table in a doctor's office, with Buzz Ramsey standing beside him.

"I should have taught you more about fistfighting and less about poker," Buzz said, worry etched deeply into his handsome face. "Who did this?"

Henry had to struggle to speak. He had never been in such pain. "A shell-game artist. An Englishman."

"Why?"

Henry told him how he had tried to walk away and how, when that out was denied, he had crushed the man's con game under his heel.

Buzz shook his head, but there was pride in his eyes when he asked, "You actually did that?"

"Yes." Henry swallowed. His lips were as thick as snakes, and his eyes were almost swollen shut. "Turns out it was a bad mistake."

"Yeah," Buzz said. "That son of a bitch almost killed you. Where did you run into him, and what did he look like?"

Henry shook his head. "If you bust your hands up on his jaw, you won't be able to play cards. We'll starve to death, between the two of us."

"What did he look like?" Buzz asked, his voice hardening with insistence.

Henry told him, adding, "I think I heard someone call his name—Cid."

"You rest easy."

"Buzz?"

He turned. "Yeah."

"Did you win at poker?"

Buzz looked away quickly. "You don't worry about things. The Englishman is going to pay the doctor's bills."

Henry closed his eyes. "He whipped me easy," he said. "Be careful, he's tough."

"He's dead," Buzz replied softly as he left the room.

Buzz found the Englishman and his friend almost in the same place that Henry had found him. The man was sipping on a bottle and conversing with his circle of friends. His ruddy-complected face was unmarked.

"Excuse me, do your friends address you as Cid?" Buzz asked with a disarming grin.

"That's bloody right, mate. And who are you?"

"A friend of that boy you half killed earlier today," Buzz said, just as conversationally as if they were about to share the bottle.

The Englishman and the gunman were of the same size—both just slightly past the prime of life. But there was something very, very deadly in Buzz Ramsey's pale blue eyes, and the Englishman back away. His hands came up and he said, "I'm not packing a gun, mate. You shoot me, you'll be lynched from a bloody telegraph pole!"

"Oh?" Buzz said. "Hmmm. I don't think I'll shoot you, then, after all. What I'll do is beat you to a bloody pulp. How would that be?"

The shell-game artist smiled; all the worry disappeared from his face. "That's a tall order, mate, and I don't think you're man enough to carry it out."

Buzz lunged and threw a straight right that connected so hard that pain shot up his forearm, and he knew he had injured a knuckle. The Englishman slammed up against the wall of the saloon and bounced off, his eyes slightly glazed but full of fight.

Buzz knew that he was in serious trouble. He had landed his best punch exactly as he had intended, and the one who appeared to have suffered the most damage was himself. That was sort of unnerving. It was even more unnerving when the man's first punch almost took his head off and drove him off the porch to land in the dirt.

Buzz rolled as the Englishman's boots stomped down where his head should have been. He jumped to his feet and charged. They came together grappling for holds, stomping at each other's ankles, and fighting to throw each other down. The Englishman was stronger. Buzz knew that within a second; and when the man drew him in and then tripped him down, Buzz was lucky to get free with only one hard punch landing on his cheek.

"Come on, mate, you're no bloody tougher than the kid!" The Englishman's blood was up, and he looked almost happy.

Buzz ducked a punch and drove his left into the Englishman's jaw. It was like punching the rock face of a wall. He backed up, both hands already injured. The Englishman advanced with a sneer on his lips.

Buzz reared back and drove his boot right up between the man's legs and made him roar with pain and grab his ruined testicles. Buzz jabbed him twice, once in each eye. When his left hand hurt even more, he whispered, "Oh, to hell with this!"

He yanked his gun out and pistol-whipped the Englishman to his knees. Clubbed him twice across the head and then slashed him across the nose, breaking it, and sending his beaten opponent pitching forward into the dirt.

Buzz, gun in hand, turned around to the spectators. "You men are big Cid's friends; if you want a piece of this fight, say so right now!"

Not one of them moved. Buzz nodded. He painfully holstered his gun, knowing he was in deep trouble now because he could not play cards professionally.

He looked down at the groaning Englishman.

"Goddamn small-time cheat," he swore. "People like you make me sick!"

With that, he drove the toe of his boot solidly into the man's ribs. The Englishman screamed and passed out. Buzz bent over and found his purse and removed all of his money.

"For the boy's medical bills," he explained. "I'm afraid you friends will have to help pay for his bills out of your own pockets."

He shoved the money in his coat pocket, and his fingers touched his own shells. He pulled them out and placed them on the palm of his right hand.

"Anyone want to play?" he asked them.

No one volunteered. "How about for just a dime? No? How about a nickel or . . . or even a penny?" His voice hardened, lashed at them like a whip. "What's the bloody matter, no bloody guts?"

They were ashamed, as he intended they should be. They had ridiculed Henry; now it was right they should be ridiculed in return.

Buzz turned around and left them with their heads hanging.

He walked back to the doctor's office and peered in at Henry, who was sleeping. He turned to the doctor and said, "How is he doing?"

"He had the great advantage of being young," the doctor said, smiling wearily. "I'm fifty-three and, if I were to take a beating like that, I don't know if I would still be alive. It gets tougher as we get older."

"Yeah," Buzz said, "I know. Doc, would you take a look at my hands?"

The doctor really looked at him. "So," he said, "you didn't take a lesson from your friend, but had to go out and get into a brawl all on your own."

"They sorta had something to do with each other," Buzz said, wincing as he touched his swollen cheek.

"Here, let me examine that."

The doctor touched the cheek, probed the jaw and cheek bones. "No fracture that I can see," he said. "But you're damned lucky."

"How about my hands? Particularly the middle knuckle on my right one." Buzz held them both out for the doctor to examine, though he figured he already knew the extent of the injuries.

"This right knuckle is severely damaged, along with both of those on either side. What we have is a lateral dislocation that will gradually work itself back into place. Are you a gunfighter or card sharp, sir?"

Buzz thought it best to own up to the truth. "I have been known to win a few hands of cards."

The doctor frowned. "And from the looks of that six-gun you are packing, I'd guess you have shot a man or two."

"Only in self-defense, Doc. Only in self-defense."

"Well," the doctor said, "I would strongly advise you against betting your life on the turn of a card or the use of a gun."

"That bad?"

"Draw your gun and attempt to cock the hammer," the doctor ordered.

When Buzz tried, he found that although he had thought his thumb was fine, just the attempt to draw back the hammer of his Colt brought immediate and excruciating pain surging through his entire right hand.

"Let's see that left one," the doctor said, "it looks pretty swollen too." He massaged it with his thumb. "That hurt?"

"Only enough to make me want to scream."

"My guess is that you have just torn a little inner tissue loose. It'll heal. Can you make a fist with both hands?"

Buzz tried and succeeded. "Can you squeeze them together?"

"I can," Buzz said, "but it's no fun. Hurts like blazes."

"Of course it does. I'll give you some liniment to rub into those hands twice a day."

"Horse liniment?"

The doctor turned and gave him a look of disgust. "Horse or man, what's the difference? The best liniments are all anti-swelling substances to keep down inflammation and to soothe the bruised tissue. By the way, I want to keep that boy here under observation for at least a couple of days and nights. He was severely beaten."

"You may get another customer in a few minutes," Buzz said, deciding that a warning was absolutely necessary. "A bloody Englishman by the name of Cid. Keep young Henry out of his sight, or someone may die yet."

"I understand. Did you . . . did you do a thorough job on him?"

"I did." Buzz peeked back in at Henry. "I broke his goddamn nose with the barrel of my sixgun and his ribs with the toe of my boot. His jaw proved too hard to do much of anything to except hurt my own fists."

The doctor nodded and rummaged through a drawer to extract a bottle of liniment. He handed it to Buzz, saying, "I could have told you that the English, Irish, and all the rest of those northern Europeans, have thick skulls."

Buzz nodded and pulled out the money he had taken from the Englishman's pockets. "How much do I owe you?"

"About twenty dollars ought to cover my services for both you and the boy. Oh yes, make that twenty-two to include his meals and the liniment."

"That takes all but fifty cents of what I have left," Buzz groused.

The doctor stepped over and took his fee out of

Buzz's hands, all except for one greenback dollar. "You keep that for a good meal. Then you go to the Consolidated Mine and ask to see a Mr. Ronald Bradley. He'll put you to work loading ore wagons down under."

"Not interested," Buzz said.

The doctor appeared not to have heard him. "Be sure and tell Ron I said you'll need to wear thick gloves. You work a week or two; it'll help realign that dislocated knuckle and also flush out the swelling, not to mention keep you clothed, fed, and with a bed to sleep in."

"I said—"

"I know what you said," the doctor grunted. "You said you were an out-of-business cardsharp and gunfighter. The gunfighter part means you need to be out of sight until you can defend yourself. You've probably stepped beyond the law, and you might even have a bounty on your head. What better place to hide than down in a mine while you earn an honest living?"

"I never thought of it quite that way," Buzz said.

"Think about it," the doctor growled. "Now get out of here before they haul the Englishman in here and we have dead people lying all over my office!"

Buzz nodded and headed for the door.

"By the way," the doctor called, stopping Buzz in his tracks. "I'm glad to know the mean son of a bitch that beat that youngster in the next room got what was coming to him. Nice work."

Buzz shook his head. "If you felt that way about it, you should have cut down on your doctorin' bill."

"I didn't feel that strongly about it, mister. Now go find the Consolidated and learn for maybe the first time in your life how it feels to earn an honest wage."

A week later, Buzz decided it didn't feel at all good to earn honest money. He worked as a scaler, a man who raked loose rock off the roofs of the tunnels before it fell on the expert miners. When the loose rock was scraped away, Buzz loaded it into wheelbarrows and hauled it up a steeply inclined tunnel. Once outside, he pushed the wheelbarrow along a board track until he reached a steep embankment, where he dumped the rock into a tailings pile. It was brutal, dangerous, and grinding work. The foreman of his shift was a hard-driving man, one who drove his men to the limit. "You there!" he bellowed. "You're moving too damned slow!"

Buzz strained to push a particularly heavy load of rock up the tunnel. He was sore and angry. This job paid just three dollars a day, and that was barely enough for food, a couple of drinks, and the small hotel room he shared with Henry. The room stunk with the smell of its grubby occupants.

The walls were paper-thin and there was only one bed, so he and Henry took turns using it. Henry was about recovered, and was talking about coming to work in the mines. Buzz had not encouraged him, for he had begun to think of traveling on to some other town. Jumbo was a hard-luck place for him, and the cards had not been turning up in his favor.

"I said move it!"

Buzz finally realized the foreman was yelling at him. It was the last straw. He set the wheelbarrow down and then shoved it over with his boot. The loose rock spilled across the narrow tunnel, momentarily blocking it and stopping the work of the other human mules like himself.

"What the hell are you doing?"

Buzz turned around and drove his gloved fist into the foreman's stomach. The man's eyes bulged and his mouth flew open. Buzz almost punched him again, in the face, but, even though his fists were gloved in heavy leather, he decided not to take the chance. So he just grabbed the bent, gasping foreman and shoved him headfirst into the tunnel wall. The man collapsed without a sound or even a quiver.

Buzz removed his gloves. He wiggled his fingers and decided that they were fine. Outside, he went to the pay shack and drew his day's wages, which amounted to only two dollars because the shift was still uncompleted.

He needed some *real* money. Enough money to pay off their mounting livery bill, buy some ammunition and supplies, and still have enough left over to take him to a fresh town and a high-stakes poker game. His luck was sure to change; it had run bad for too long now.

Buzz heard the mine's steam whistle blow one hour before the new shifts were to come on. The whistles were shrill and could be heard for miles. Buzz had come to hate them. He decided it was time to leave Jumbo.

On his way back to the hotel, he stopped across the street from the Nevada Bank and stared at it thoughtfully. He had not been inside the place, so he walked over to it and opened the door for a woman and then stepped inside. The bank looked prosperous. There were oriental rugs on the floor, polished brass railings, and cuspidors so fancy you weren't even supposed to spit into them.

Three male cashiers were handling three lines of miners, who were making deposits of both gold and cash.

"Excuse me," Buzz said to one of the waiting men. "How long does this place stay open?"

The man said, "Until five o'clock. About another half-hour is all."

"Thank you."

Buzz stepped back outside and walked quickly to the hotel, where he found Henry. "Get ready to leave," he said, taking his holstered sixgun out of his bedroll and strapping it around his waist. "Meet me at the livery in about twenty minutes and have the horses ready to ride."

"What about the livery bill?"

"It'll be paid."

"Where are you going?" Henry demanded.

Buzz lied. "I won a big pot of money today playing stud poker, and the man is trying to figure a way out of honoring his IOUs. I plan to change his thinking on that score."

"Maybe I can help you."

"No." Buzz turned at the doorway. "Just be saddled and ready in case there is trouble and the man has a bunch of friends. Okay?"

Henry nodded, with reluctance. It was clear he was worried about his friend. His face was still a little swollen and purplish.

Buzz smiled and totally disarmed Henry's fears. "Better get moving fast, kid. Some men can be pretty sore losers."

"All right."

Buzz closed the door and inspected his sixgun. Satisfied that it was ready for anything, he headed for the Bank of Nevada, checking his pocket watch as soon as he hit the street. He wanted to be at their doorstep right at closing time.

And that is exactly how he timed it. A bank clerk was at the door, pulling out his keys to lock up, when Buzz pushed by him and settled in at the very end of the line. It was fifteen minutes after five when he stepped up to the cashier's cage. He was the bank's last customer of the day.

"What will it be, sir?" the cashier, a young, harried-looking man, asked.

"Cash," Buzz replied. "I'd like to make a large cash withdrawal."

"I see. And your name?"

"Colt." Buzz said softly as he drew his sixgun and eased it onto the marbletop counter. He covered it with the thick arm of his sheepskin-lined jacket. "And Colt promises that, if you make one warning sound to the others in this room, you'll be a dead man."

The cashier paled. He started to look around for help, but Buzz's whispered warning froze him. "Don't! Just empty your drawer and put all your three biggest denominations directly in front of me. No one even has to know until I'm gone."

The cashier seemed to get a grip on his fear. He emptied three drawers of greenbacks and whispered, "Do you want a sack?"

"No, thank you."

Buzz smiled at the cashier as he stuffed the money into his big coat pockets. "Have a good day," he said cheerfully as he slid his sixgun into his coat sleeve and backed toward the doorway, leaving no doubt in the cashier's mind that he would draw and fire his gun if an alarm was sounded before he was gone.

"Have a nice evening," Buzz said to the bank employee who was waiting impatiently at the door to lock it for the final time.

"Thank you," the man said without warmth.

Buzz backed through the doorway, turned, and took three long strides before he heard the cashier scream, "Holdup! Get him!"

He threw himself into a narrow alley and ran for his life. A gun boomed and a bullet whipped past his ear. It made him run even faster.

He skidded around the corner into the alley, scattering a pile of rubbish and a pair of alleycats who had been feeding. He raced down the alley. More gunshots chased him. Then he doubled back to the main street and lost himself in the crowds until he reached the livery.

"Are you ready?" he called when he saw Henry.

"Yeah, but this man won't release our horses until we pay our feed and board bill."

Buzz hurried over to a smallish but very determined little man. "How much is the damage?"

"Sixteen dollars."

"Here's twenty," Buzz said, pulling a handful of greenbacks out of his coat pocket. "Keep the change."

The little man's entire countenance changed almost as if by magic. He stared at the money and beamed. "Well, thank you, sir!"

Buzz vaulted onto his horse and sank his heels into the animal's ribs. It jumped forward and galloped out of the barn. Buzz turned it right, yelling, "Come on, Henry! Time's a-wastin'!"

As he raced across the main street, Buzz looked in the direction of the holdup. He saw a big crowd in front of the Bank of Nevada, people running around in confusion. Then the sight was lost as his horse carried him down a side street, with Henry right behind, yelling, "Where are we going?"

"Any place is fine with me, as long as it's far from here!"

Chapter 9

Jessie and Ki reached the valley where the Slades had attacked the Crow. The temperature was not much above freezing, and a steady wind from the north promised fresh snow. They weren't thinking about the cold or the approaching storm, but instead about the tracks they saw leading into the valley.

"Something went wrong for the Slades," Ki said as they dismounted and stood beside the trees.

"Yes," Jessie agreed, leading Sun back and forth and trying to read the tracks. "Right over here is where the Slades waited in the forest to attack."

"But why would they be so foolish?" Ki asked. "We were told that there were a hundred Crow warriors. Even with superior arms, it does not seem possible that they could have beaten the Indians."

"Unless they thought they had them caught by surprise."

"Let's ride down into that valley and see if they had any success," Ki said, his expression doubtful.

When Jessie and Ki reached the valley floor, the most obvious thing they saw were the many half-dug depressions that marked the valley floor. Jessie puzzled over them. "Why do you suppose they dug these?"

Ki knelt beside the shallow indentations, then walked around the Indian camp and noted how each had been confined by the perimeter of the tipi marked by pole marks and the flattened winter grass. "The squaws must have scooped these out and lain in them during the attack while the warriors waited until the Slades had emptied their rifles. Then, the Indians struck swiftly." He pointed across the valley. "Look out over there. *That's* where we'd find whatever is left of the Slades."

Jessie saw a low depression at the far end of the valley. And now, she saw the wolves. "Ki, we'll find nothing but bones gnawed by wolves." She shuddered a little. "Do you think they were *all* killed?"

Ki jumped back onto his horse. "I'll have the answer to that in a few minutes."

As he galloped off, Jessie stared at the scene of the battle. Now that she understood the reason for the shallow depressions, she could almost close her mind and see how the battle would have gone. The Crow had simply outwitted them. So great must Napolean Slade's hatred of the Indians have been that he had even lost sense of his purpose and been willing to sacrifice the life of his daughter, Maud. And that same blinding hatred had cost him his entire famiily.

Ki returned. His expression was very bleak. "At least two of the Slades escaped. Their shod horses broke through a second line of Indians hiding across the valley. They escaped into the mountains."

"Could they have survived?"

"I don't know," the samurai admitted. "I followed their tracks for a few miles. The Indians were right behind them. But I have a feeling they might have escaped. From the looks of the horses I saw back at their ranch, the Slades were mounted on better horses than the Indians could be expected to own. They were a pretty well-to-do family."

"I know," Jessie said. "But imagine how many people they killed, cheated, or frightened in gaining their land and position." She shook her head and toed the upturned earth. "Well, all that changed right here in this valley. I guess the question now is, what will the four survivors do? Will they continue to hunt down Buzz Ramsey . . . or give it up?"

"You would be the better judge of that," Ki said. "You have always been able to guess the workings of the American mind better than I."

Had the circumstances been pleasanter, Jessie might have smiled at that comment. But here in this valley of death, she felt crowded by ghosts and wanted nothing more than to ride away quickly.

"My guess is the pair that escaped went on to find Buzz Ramsey. They had vowed to kill him, and I think that, after this disaster, they will hold that vow even more dearly."

"That doesn't seem logical to me," the samurai said.

"I know. But men like Napoleon Slade base their whole lives on bullying and threats. If they make one publicly and fail, then they will perceive themselves as weak and vulnerable to others."

"But almost the entire family was wiped out here!"

"They still have land and cattle. Probably money enough in the bank to buy more winter hay to replace that which we burned. There are dozens of out-of-work cowboys in Cheyenne who will hire on for not much more than bed and board. And some of them will be cut of the same cloth as the Slades."

Jessie took a deep breath. "Ki, you aren't going to like this, but we've come to a fork in the trail."

"What do you mean?"

"I mean that we have to split up right now. You have to go after Candace. I'm going after the two Slades who escaped this death-trap, before their trail is lost.

Ki's face darkened. "I think we should stay together."

"If we do that, either Candace or Henry will have to be sacrificed. I can't make the choice, can you?"

The samurai gritted his teeth and turned away for a moment to compose his face. His choice was always for Jessie Starbuck. But he understood her reasoning. If they abandoned the trail of the Slades, that deadly pair might find Ramsey and ambush him *and* Henry Whitman. And if they both followed the Slades, Candace Whitman was lost.

Jessie placed her hand on Ki's shoulder. "All I've got to do is warn Buzz and Henry of the threat. I'm asking you to do a far more dangerous job, Ki. I'm asking you to somehow rescue Candace Whitman from the Crow and return her safely to Circle Star."

The samurai stood very still. His mind worked at the problem furiously, but he could see no possible way that he and Jessie could save both the boy and his mother if they rode together. Jessie was right. But it almost killed the samurai to think of her tracking the Slades, who were, in turn, being pursued by Indians. Jessie had made it sound as if there was no threat to her own life. That was definitely not true. She was embarking on a terribly dangerous journey, one on which he would not be available to help.

"Ki," she whispered, "I want you to know something. If I wasn't sure that this was the only way to save those two, I wouldn't suggest it.

"I'm not worried about myself. With Sun, I can outrun any Indians that I might chance upon in these mountains. And I have a rifle that I know how to use. Father taught me how to survive in the wilderness. I'll be all right." She smiled. "It's you that I am most worried about."

He blinked. "Me?"

"Yes. I'm worried that you will become so concerned about *my* safety that you will neglect your own. I don't know how you intend to free Candace, but guard your own life dearly."

"I will," he said in a tight voice. "Go now. I will see you again at the Circle Star."

"Yes," Jessie whispered as she mounted Sun and stared across this valley of death. "I will see you in Texas."

Ki watched her leave. It was the hardest thing he had ever done in his life. If that woman were killed by the Slades or the Crow Indians chasing them, he would hunt down her killers and slaughter them . . . before he would commit *seppuku* and end his own miserable life.

He stood very still beside his horse until Jessie had vanished across the valley and into the forest. Then, the samurai turned his face north and swung lightly into his saddle. His horse, a pinto gelding strong of wind and leg, was weary from the hard, long miles they had already ridden up from Texas. But the animal had long ago been chosen for its heart and stamina. Ki knew the pinto would run until it dropped dead. But he would not ask such a sacrifice until it became absolutely necessary. Until he had Candace Whitman and was fleeing from the Indians.

That same day of their parting, Ki had ridden straight into a snowstorm. After several hours, he had been forced to take refuge in the forest to avoid freezing to death. The storm blew for two days, and there wasn't a single minute that he did not worry about Jessica Starbuck and wonder if she had found a low, sheltered place. Ki alternately fretted and chided himself for worrying about what could not be changed. Besides, Jessie had been telling the truth. Old Alex Starbuck had been a financial genius and a tycoon, but he had also been a survivor—both in the business world and the outdoors. He had taught Jessie very well.

Jessie would make it.

When the storm finally broke, the sun came out and the temperature warmed considerably. The snow melted, and Ki traveled as fast as he dared push his gelding. The trail of the huge Crow village was easy to follow, and though it was more than a week old, Ki steadily gained on the Indians. With tipi, squaws and children, the Crow were moving slowly. Because of their numbers, their only real threat of attack was from their traditional enemies, the Bannock, Flatheads, and the fearsome Sioux, who had dominated the Great Plains like the Tartars of Russia.

Ki finally overtook the Crow village near the confluence of the Yellowstone and the Bighorn River. Had he not been wary and kept a close watch on the trail ahead without ever allowing himself to be skylighted, the Crow would have detected him on their backtrail. But he traveled in forest, even when there was open country much easier to cross. And because of this, he topped a mountain and looked out to see the great rivers merging in the distance, and the huge camp of the Crow.

They must have been joined by another band of their tribe. Ki spent almost an hour studying the big field of tipis. He estimated that there were at least three thousand Indians encamped in the valley.

That made things extremely difficult. With that many people, dogs, and horses, it was going to take some time just to locate Candace Whitman, and only then he could attempt a rescue.

The samurai sat cross-legged under the snow-laden boughs of a big pine tree. Behind him, the pinto munched at brown, frozen grass, which the samurai had laboriously uncovered in order that the animal's strength be maintained.

Three days later, and always from a different position, the samurai waited. His eyes burned and were swollen red from staring down into the snow-covered land. He had located Maud Slade early on the second day, but it had taken him until this morning to pick out Candace, who mostly remained inside a tipi. But now they were both outside, though at opposite sides of the camp. They were too far away to distinguish clearly, yet he could tell from their shapes and the way they moved that they were not Indian women.

Candace and Maud Slade were very dissimilar in build. Candace was lithe, almost girlish, and Ki guessed she was even more slender than he remembered her to be. In contrast, Maud was man-sized, big shouldered, and though no longer fat, she walked like a man, and he would surely have mistaken her for one had she not been wearing a dirty calico dress. They were with a large group of women, cooking.

Ki closed his eyes, and they bled painful tears due to irritation. He could rest them occasionally, for there only remained the question of where each of the women were being kept.

It was funny. Not until the moment that he had seen Maud Slade had he given any consideration to rescuing her from the Crow. But now he knew that he had to at least give it a try, even though it would probably double the risk of failure. Ki's fight was with the Slade men, not their women.

That decided, he opened his eyes every five minutes until the day grew late and the sun began to go down. Then the glare was gone, and he watched the Indian camp prepare to settle in for the night.

Meals were cooked, buffalo-robe coats were donned, and the camp gradually moved inside the tipis. To Ki's great disappointment, the two white women did not move any closer. Maud entered a tipi almost fifty yards away from the one that Candace disappeared into.

Dammit! Ki stood up and moved to the base of the pine tree, where his dark clothes would blend with the bark until the sun set and darkness covered the land.

I will get Candace first, he thought, *and then, if it seems reasonable, I will make a try for the Slade woman.*

Ki studied both tipis until he knew that he would be able to swiftly find and identify them at night. Because of a three-quarter moon and the snow, vision would be almost too good. He would have preferred less moon and more darkness.

Ki returned to his horse and opened his saddlebags. He found his *ninja* costume, a form-fitting black suit with a hood that covered his head except for narrow eye slits. In Japan, old Kobi-San had spent years teaching him *kyusutsu, kenjutsu, bojutsu* and *shuriken-jutsu,* the arts of bow and arrow, sword, staff, and throwing-blade, along with the other fighting arts. Ki was a legitimate master of all of them, and would have held his own with any martial-arts expert in the Land of the Rising Sun.

But of all the arts, it was *ninjutsu,* the "art of the invisible assassin," that the old *ronin* had stressed to his young pupil. The *ninja* were the most feared of all warriors. They were professional assassins, men who killed for money and could not be taken alive. They could steal into palaces which were guarded by thousands of samurai warriors, and kill their chosen quarry. They spent their entire existences training for the role of taking or giving—if necessary—human life.

And now, as the samurai moved down from the forest to the valley, he was a *ninja.* Only instead of assassination, his mind and his body were totally committed to the act of rescuing two women, women that he hardly knew at all but for whom he would die, if necessary, to save them from a life of slavery among the Crow Indians.

He could not be a *ninja* leading his pinto, so he gave the matter no more thought. It did occur to him that he would have to steal horses in order to have any chance of getting the two women away alive.

Ki moved like a shadow across the land. It was easy for him, a samurai trained to sneak across an open, sunlit courtyard without detection. But the fact that he had an entire field of trees, shrubs, and then humanity to blend into did not diminish his care or enormous concentration.

To begin with, he had to approach the camp without arousing the Indian dogs, animals whose specific function it was to warn the village of any approaching dangers.

This Ki was able to do. So cleanly did he dart from shadow to shadow that he passed silently into the village without a single dog barking to warn of his approach.

Now he found a blanket and wrapped it around his *ninja* costume, because there were dogs throughout the camp, and even though he could pass unseen among them, his own foreign scent would set off a chorus of alarm. Ki covered his head with the blanket and walked boldly among the tents. The buffalo-skin tipis were thick and warm. He could hear their occupants talking around their campfires, hear children laughing and crying, a mother's sharp scolding. It was funny: had this been a city of whites and he been walking through a town, he would have heard the same sounds of families gathering for the evening meal and preparing for the night's sleep.

The aroma of cooking meat filled the samurai's nostrils and made his empty belly twist with sharp displeasure. He had not eaten well since leaving Jessica, using only enough food to husband his strength for the task that she had assigned him.

A few Indians moved in the camp. Head down, Ki did not acknowledge them as he walked steadily toward the tipi that held Candace Whitman. When he reached it, he turned full circle to study the route he would take to find Maud Slade.

He could hear voices inside, and guessed that there were at least three adult Indians in addition to Candace. Ki took a deep breath. He flung the robe down beside the entrance, and without any hesitation, burst inside.

There, he found three old squaws sitting on buffalo robes. They were circled around the fire, eating, while Candace was back against the opposite wall. She saw and recognized him first; being young, her reaction was swiftest—and that might have saved their lives. Candace jumped at one of the squaws and covered her mouth. Ki had not expected women; rather, he had anticipated warriors. His adjustment to the discovery was that, instead of using killing force, the samurai used two quick knife-hand blows to their necks. The squaws folded over, unconscious.

But the one that Candace had grabbed bit her hand. Candace gasped with pain, yet had the presence of mind not to yell. In two seconds, the rock-hard edge of the samurai's hand flashed once more, and the old squaw released her bite and slumped over.

"You!" Candace whispered. "Why you?"

"I was the only one in these parts interested in getting you out of here," Ki said. "Get your things; we are getting out of here."

Candace did not waste time with idle talk. She grabbed a buffalo robe and a bag of something and said, "I don't think there is a chance of escape, but I'll die with you, trying."

Outside again, Ki grabbed the same Indian robe he had used to cross the emcampment. He wrapped it around his shoulders, then started across the camp to get Maud.

It seemed as though the journey across that hundred yards took years. In fact, it took less than five minutes. When they reached the right tipi, Ki held up a finger to his lips and whispered, "Wait right here. Don't move, don't make a sound."

_"But . . . but what . . ."

The samurai dropped the blanket and ducked inside the tipi. He was going to get the Slade woman and then they'd get horses and . . .

Maud Slade was cooking and a big Indian warrior was eating. When Maud looked up and saw the samurai, she did what he should have guessed she might do the moment she saw a man in a black *ninja* outfit leaping into her tipi. She shouted a warning that could have been heard in Canada, then she grabbed the pot of food she was cooking and slung it in Ki's face.

Blinded, he staggered. Then the warrior *and* the white woman were on him. Ki got his feet tangled up in a buffalo robe, and fell. The scalding food had blinded him, and when his eyes cleared, he looked up to see the warrior grabbing a war axe to chop at his head. Ki ducked. The axe whistled overhead. The samurai struck the Indian in the throat, and the man gagged and his face went purple.

"Aheeeeiiii!" Maud screamed as she threw herself on Ki with all the passion of a mother grizzly. "Aheeiiii!"

"Shut up," Ki grunted, trying to fend off her spirited attack. "I'm a white man, come to save you!"

But the crazy woman screamed even louder. Her mouth was wide open. Ki slapped her and she shut up, but then she doubled her fist and drove it into his face. "Get out of my tipii!" she roared. "Get out! Aheeiii!"

Ki had enough. He whirled and dashed outside, but it was too late. A dozen Crow warriors had Candace and him trapped. There was no escape. Only failure and certain death.

★

Chapter 10

"Don't move!" Candace whispered. "Don't even blink."

Ki stood very still. He supposed that, had he been armed, they would have shot him the instant he stepped outside the tent. But standing open-handed, they did not know how lethal his hands and feet were, and they had no fear of him whatsoever. They did not know that he carried his *tanto* blade under his *ninja* costume and his *shuriken* star-blades sewed inside the linings of his tunic. If they raised their weapons, Ki vowed, he was going to take a lot of them with him.

Candace began to talk rapidly in sign language. It was a universal language used by all western tribes and, had Ki not been standing directly behind her, he probably could have understood something of what she was saying. But it was hopeless now and the woman had warned him not to move, so he just stood there and watched the Indians to gauge their reaction.

Their reaction was not good. Suddenly, a big, strong-looking warrior slammed his palm with a clenched fist and shouted something in anger. He started to grab Candace and pull her to him, but she shouted back and grabbed Ki around his body and hugged him tightly.

"Don't just stand there like a tree; hug me back!" she whispered urgently.

Ki hugged her. The big warrior roared with anger, and Ki said, "Whatever we are supposed to be doing, it isn't working."

"I told him you were my husband and I was your wife. I told him I would rather die than leave you and that, if you were sacrificed, I wanted to be killed too."

"Are you crazy?"

"Shhh!" Candace said, making more signs that Ki guessed were to emphasize her determined stand. "Just let me do the talking."

"I have no choice," Ki said. "But you sure aren't making any friends. And—"

"I saw you fight at Delgado's stage station, remember?"

"I remember I didn't do any better there than I've done here so far."

"Eight men jumped you all at once. Besides, Jessie told me that you were trained a samurai, and samurai are the world's greatest fighters. Is that true or not?"

"We try," he answered. "But these Crow look pretty mean themselves, and there are six of them, and more on the way."

That part of it was true enough. The entire village was emerging from their tipis and hurrying over to see what was causing such a disturbance. When they saw Ki, they fell grim and silent as they listened to the big warrior and Candace argue in sign and an occasional word or two of Crow.

"Buffalo Runner," Candace said in English. The chief scowled but he nodded, his eyes never leaving the samurai. Again, by using sign language and grabbing Ki, she indicated that he was her man and she was his woman. Buffalo Runner's scowl darkened and he pointed to a huge warrior whose name was Big Elk. When he grabbed Candace and tried to pull her toward the warrior, she grabbed a knife from one of the squaws standing close by, and she pressed it to her own throat hard enough to make a thin trickle of blood flow.

The Crow Indians fell silent. They seemed very impressed by the white woman's commitment to slit her own throat rather than be separated from her husband. Ki too was impressed, and he understood that this was a bold gamble that did not dare fail. Candace had probably decided death would be preferable to marrying the huge Crow warrior.

Maud Slade had it figured entirely different. Now, as she came outside of the tipi and sized up the situation, she pushed between the big warrior and Candace. "Chief," she said to Buffalo Runner, and then she went into sign language too rapid for Ki to follow. Maud had been with the Crow for a considerably longer period of time than Candace and she could also speak a fair number of Crow words, which she liberally interspersed with her sign language.

Finally, the chief threw up his hands in a gesture of exasperation and nodded with apparent reluctance.

Maud blew out her fat cheeks and expelled a deep sigh of relief. "I just saved your ass, Chinaman. And yours too, Candace."

"Thank you," Candace said. "What are they going to do to us?"

"Tomorrow, the Chinaman will have to fight every warrior in the tribe who wants you for his squaw. Big Elk has first claim, but the line forms right after him, and it's pretty damn long. I don't understand that. My own warrior, Short Dog, was the only one that saw my considerable worth, bless his horny little heart."

"You *like* being married to him?"

"Why sure! I snapped him into shape, and he ain't run off every time I kicked his big ass for stepping out of line. I'm getting right fond of him. And, according to Crow law, if he gets killed in a battle, his brother has to take me as his wife. And his brother is a good-lookin' buck for damned certain! Sure beats being a widow."

Candace just stared. Her disbelief must have been quite evident, because Maud added shortly, "Listen, honey, when you're as loud, fat, and ugly as me, you got to take what you can and be grateful. Yeah, I had a big house outside of Cheyenne, and a whole passel of pigs to feed and clean up after. They cussed me and woulda worked me into an early grave if I'd stayed among 'em."

"But the Crow killed your family!"

Maud clenched her fists. "And my family," she gritted, "riddled every damned tipi in the whole village, knowing full well I was probably inside one of them! To hell with Pa and the rest! They got what they deserved when they tried to slaughter all these women and children. Made me sick to my stomach, and I don't get sick easy. I didn't waste a single minute in mourning a damn one of the blood thirsty bastards, and I'm sorry that Pa and Jethro, the meanest of the lot, got plumb away."

"What happens if I lose tomorrow?" Ki asked.

"When you do lose, which you probably will right away because Big Elk is a wicked fighter, then he gets Candace. If you kill him, then the next and the next Indian brave will fight you until one of them takes your scalp—which they seem real impressed with, Chinaman."

"And the weapons?"

"Knives."

"I have my own inside this *ninja* costume."

"Your what?"

"This . . . this black outfit that I'm wearing."

Maud scowled. "I never saw the likes of you, mister. Neither have the Crow. They been asking me how you got past their dogs."

"I used the skills I was taught as a samurai."

Maud didn't know or care what a samurai was. "Then you snuck past them?"

"Yes."

"Too bad," Maud said, clucking her tongue, "for the dogs. We'll be eating the lot of them over the next few weeks."

"I want to stay with Ki," Candace said.

"You can," Maud said. "That's part of the deal I struck. Tonight, he is still your man. But tomorrow, you're the same as up for grabs. And the warrior that gets you, beds you."

Candace shuddered with dread.

Maud touched her arm sympathetically. "They ain't so bad, these Indians. They don't get drunk 'cause there's nothing to drink. They don't beat their wives— not that Short Dog could whip me anyway. Most of 'em are a damn sight cleaner than the menfolk I'm used to. And if you keep 'em warm and satisfied in bed, they'll love you up real fine."

"If I have to marry one, I'll put the knife back to my throat, and I'll use it!"

Maud shook her head and then shrugged her round shoulders. "You got to do what you got to do, Candace, but life's short enough as it is without putting an abrupt end to it all by yourself."

Ki said, "I'll need food and rest if I'm to fight like a samurai tomorrow for you." The air was very cold and he was weary and hungry.

Candace nodded. She turned to the chief and made the universal sign of hunger and sleep. The chief nodded and shouted orders. A moment later, a squaw beckoned.

"Samawry!" Maud shouted.

Ki turned.

"Don't you try to escape tonight. They'll have guards all around your tipi. I gave my word you were a man of

123

honor, not to mention not a total fool. And if you try to escape I'll pay with *my* life."

Ki cursed inwardly, for it had certainly been his intention to try to escape if there had been any way to take Candace with him. But now he was bound by honor to remain and fight.

"You have my word as a samurai I will not try to escape," he solemnly pledged.

Maud nodded. "I can tell you set big store by that 'samawry' thing. I'll sleep easy after I finish with Short Dog tonight."

The big, fat, ugly woman giggled. Ki smiled. He sort of liked her, which came as a surprise.

They were led to a tipi, where the squaw opened the flap and gestured for them to go inside. She was huffy and followed them in, then pointed toward a large pot of stew that was simmering on her campfire. There was also some kind of bread. The squaw was very upset. She gesticulated wildly and, because she had no front teeth, spittle drooled down her many chins. Finally satisfied that she had expressed her great displeasure that the two white captives should be lodged in her tipi, she scooped up the finest of her buffalo robes and left them alone.

"She wasn't too pleased about this arrangement, was she?" Ki said.

"I would say that was an understatement," Candace said, closing the flap to keep the tipi from losing its heat.

Ki knelt down and tasted the stew, using a wooden ladle. Either he was so hungry that he had lost all sense of taste, or else the stew was delicious. Ki chose to think it delicious. "There's only one bowl," he said. "Eat first. I will follow."

"I have already eaten," she said. "And you must eat all of the stew and the bread."

"Are you sure?" The woman seemed a little drawn, and Ki felt she could use some additional weight.

Candace nodded.

"All right," he decided. "I will eat the stew and half of the bread. But you must eat the rest."

"Tell me the truth, Ki. How much of a chance do you really have?" she asked when he had finished his meal and sat cross-legged before the fire. "Don't exaggerate it. I expect no more than death."

"I'll make you a promise in return for promise," Ki said. When the woman did not answer, he continued, "I'll promise to fight with all of my skill and heart if you promise me that you will not take your own life if I fail and am killed."

"I can't do that."

Ki frowned. "Candace. Even if I fail, other men will come for you. Jessie knows you are here among the Crow Indians. She would never allow you to remain a slave of these people."

"I wouldn't be a slave. I'd be the wife of a Crow warrior."

"Against your free will," Ki said. "That means you are a captive."

He reached out and touched her cheek. "You have a son. Jessie has gone to take him away from Buzz Ramsey before he comes to a bad end. I remember your son very well. Henry is a fine boy. He lost his father this year; must you also take your life and rob him of a mother?"

Candace blinked. Maybe she had not thought it out all the way. But now, as Ki's words sank in, she seemed to realize that she had an obligation to live for her son, if not herself. "You are right," she told him. "Henry is almost a man now, but even men sometimes need their mothers."

Ki smiled. "You are still young and pretty, Candace.

You will have your choice among men when you return to your own people. You will remarry and live a full and happy life."

Tears welled up in her eyes and a sob escaped from her bosom. She threw her arms around the samurai and held him tightly. She was shivering, though he was not sure whether it was from cold or the fear of what tomorrow would bring.

"Hold me all night," she whispered. "I need your strength so much. I've never had anyone speak to me the truths that you have spoken. Please hold me and love me, Ki!"

"Are you sure?"

She nodded. "If . . . if it would not take away any of your great strength."

He laughed softly. His belly was full and he had no fear of death or even of failure. To a samurai, there was no dishonor in dying in battle. It was expected, even hoped, that a samurai's life would end that way. Much better to take the quick, clean thrust of a blade to the heart than slowly waste away with time. Much better! And now that Candace had pledged not to take her own life, his conscience on that matter was very clear.

"Ki?"

Her face was close to his own, and when their lips met, Ki felt heat rise in his loins. He had not had a woman in months, and this might be his very last opportunity. Maybe Candace Whitman sensed that too and wanted to give him the only thing she had left to give. Ki only knew that, no matter how complex her motives, he saw the flame of desire flicker in her eyes, and he knew she wanted him for her own pleasure.

He stood up and pulled off the *ninja* costume so that he was wearing only his cache-sex, a broad cotton band wrapped around his waist and brought up under his crotch.

Candace admired his lean, smooth, muscled body.

126

"You really are a beautiful man," she said quietly. "Tell me, samurai, what is that which you are wearing called?"

He told her. She nodded and began to undress.

"I'm afraid you will think me unattractive. I'm not so young anymore, and I'm much too thin. I—"

Ki did not let her go on. He pulled the cloth band free and let his cache-sex fall. "Look at me," he commanded. "All of me."

She looked down and saw that he was already very aroused and that his manhood was huge and throbbing.

She swallowed noisily and then was quick to slip out of the soiled dress, and the pantalettes she wore underneath. When she removed the last garments and stood before him fully unclothed, she stepped back and said, "Now, samurai, look at me."

"I am," he said. "And I would not trade the sight of you for any woman. Come here."

She smiled and flung herself into his arms. Their naked bodies locked together in an embrace for a moment. Ki lifted her off the ground and she hopped lightly up to straddle his hips. Wide open now, he allowed his stiff rod to slip into her eager wetness.

Candace arched her back. She moaned and her eyes closed as he pushed himself even deeper into her. "Ohhhh," she whispered, shivering in his arms, tightening her shapely legs around his hips and pushing herself harder up against him. "Ohhh, Ki! I've never had a man like you before!"

He bent his head and kissed her neck. His powerful legs were planted like the stumps of trees, and they looked like some carved statue of carnal pleasure in a pose that ensured the continuation of the human race.

"My dear samurai," she cooed, her breath coming fast and warm in his long, black hair, "this is using all your strength. Put me down on the buffalo robe and let me use *my* strength on you."

127

The samurai agreed. He knelt beside the fire and rolled over onto his back. Candace pulled her knees up beside his ribs and then straightened. She began to rock back and forth on his thick rod. Her face was lovely in the firelight, and her hair hung long and golden. Ki reached down and slipped his forefinger into her wetness and began to flick at her bud of desire.

Almost immediately, Candace's slender body began to jerk on his thick staff. Her slick honey-pot flowed with woman's juices, and then she moaned loudly and fell forward as her body lost control of itself and began to jerk up and down.

Ki grabbed her buttocks and drove himself up into her hard.

"Ohhhhh, ugggh! Don't stop!" she begged as she collapsed on him.

Ki rolled her over on the buffalo robe. He bent his head, and his mouth closed over her small but very firm breasts. He could feel her heart flutter like a small, captive bird trying to escape its cage. He could hear her breath coming faster again, and as he rotated his hips over her in a slow, deep stroke, he felt her womanhood come to life again and its muscles begin to work and pull at him with urgency.

"I don't . . . I can't do it again so soon. I—"

Ki closed his mouth, shutting off her words, drowning her with sensation and pleasure. She moaned and reached down to grab his powerful buttocks. She dug her fingernails into them and pulled him in to the hilt. Her legs shot straight out and her heels drummed on the tipi floor.

"Take me soon, please!" she groaned. "I never had it so long and hard."

The samurai raised up on his elbows. He looked down at the woman and watched her tongue as it darted in and out between her glistening lips. Her eyelids were quivering, and he knew that he must finish with her soon or she might faint.

"All right," he said. "With pleasure!"

Now he began to drive into her faster and harder. She clutched at him, kissing his face and neck. Her hands were moving up and down his long, sinewy back. The fire beside them seemed suddenly to grow hotter. Slick with perspiration, their bodies made quick, sucking sounds as Ki drove into her, feeling her coming again and hurrying to meet her at the same moment of ecstacy.

She began to wail, softly and faintly. Her legs lost control of themselves, and then she was bucking wildly as he slammed his hips into her again and again and spewed his seed deep into her in great torrents.

Candace could not stop moaning and whimpering until long after he lay spent on her.

"You were good," he said, finally. "Better than good. You are very much worth fighting for, even dying for tomorrow."

When she could catch her breath, she wrapped him up with her legs and arms and said, "My samurai, I could have died just now and felt I had gone to heaven. Why don't you try to kill me again and again with that big sword of yours that I have sheathed so neatly?"

"I will," he promised. "But first, I'll sleep for an hour and then wake you with desire."

They pulled the buffalo robe over them and lay watching the fire. But the samurai had been wrong about the timing—she was after him again in only twenty minutes.

He awoke to the sound of beating drums and the feel of the woman stroking his manhood one last time. Ki laced his fingers behind his head and allowed her to arouse him slowly, then impale herself with exquisite slowness. He let her work herself up into a passionate frenzy; then he rolled her over and brought her to a shuddering climax.

Candace clung to him with all her might. There were tears in her eyes when she said, "I keep pretending that, if I just refuse to let you go out there and fight, they will leave us be. Just let us stay inside here and make love forever."

Ki gently pried her arms and legs from around his body. "It doesn't work that way," he said gently. "We can't hide from those people, and the fighting won't go away by pretending. I have to go out there this morning."

He sat up and dressed. He inspected the razorlike edge of his *tanto* blade, then slid it back into its lacquered wooden sheath. "I think I had better leave this with you," he said. "Just in case."

Her eyes widened with alarm. "But I don't understand."

"If I allow a Crow warrior to kill me, then I lose. But I also lose if I kill them. What I must do is win, but without shedding Indian blood."

"But how?"

"My way of fighting is called *te*," he explained. "In your language, the word roughly translates to mean 'hand.' Have you ever heard of a place called Okinawa?"

Candace shook her head.

"It is an island—a chain of islands, really. They lie off the Japanese mainland. The Okinawans are proud people, who were once conquered by my own people and forbidden the honor of owning weapons. Any weapons at all, if found on the body of an Okinawan or in his home, would result in his death and the death of his entire family."

"Your people would do that?" Candace was appalled.

Ki nodded. "It is the Japanese way, and it would take me all winter to even attempt to explain why that is so.

It just is. Anyway, being a proud people, the Okinawans had to develop *te*, or hand fighting.

"And they became very, very good at it. So good that a master of the martial arts is more dangerous just using his hands than many men are using a gun."

"That's . . . that's incredible."

Ki smiled tolerantly. "I know. To an American, it seems impossible. Yet it is true. You must understand that the Okinawans did not devise *te* in a year or even an entire decade. It took generations, the best part of a century. But now, for a martial-arts master like myself, the body is the ultimate weapon. A gun will jam. It will misfire and quickly empty itself. But the body, that will never fail its master if it is taken care of and if the mind is its equal. Mind and body, Candace. That is the secret."

She swallowed and nodded. "I have seen what you can do to a woman with your body. But I am so afraid that—"

He silenced her with a kiss. "Don't let fear poison whatever time we have on this earth. What is to be, is to be. Worry will change nothing. Let the future take care of the future."

Ki finished dressing. He did not want them to have to come for him, so he stepped outside. He was still in his *ninja* costume, but the hood was removed and he wore black slippers with hard bamboo bottoms.

It was very cold outside and his costume was thin, yet its color absorbed the sun's warmth. He knelt outside the tipi and bowed his head and began to meditate. He immersed himself in peaceful thoughts that enhanced rather than diminished his fighting ability, because the meditation dissolved all anger from his mind and replaced it with the knowledge that his life was like a flowing river, going where it was supposed to be going. And what was required was simply that he not resist, but rather accept whatever came as natural and

131

right. Even the warriors who beat the drums and prepared themselves for deadly combat and dreamed of having his magnificent scalp were in harmony with his *karma*.

Candace touched him lightly on the shoulder. "Ki, the drums have stopped beating and the entire village is staring at you."

Ki awakened from his thoughts and opened his eyes to see seven warriors in war paint standing in a line before him. Chief Buffalo Runner came forward. The chief gestured for Ki to arise and follow him. Ki did as he was told.

At the east end of the camp, they had fashioned a circle of rocks about twenty-five feet across. In a very few gestures, the chief made it clear that the fighting was to be done inside the circle. He looked at Ki closely. Then, deciding that the samurai was unarmed, he reached into the pocket of his buffalo coat and produced a long hunting knife which he held out to Ki.

"No," the samurai said, with a quick shake of his head.

"Take it, you crazy goddamn Chinaman!" Maud shouted. "Or the Big Elk will peel your skin off like he would bark off a switch."

"No," Candace said. "Ki needs nothing but his hands."

"Oh fer Chrissakes!" Maud swore. "You've gone as crazy as the samawry."

Candace lost her temper. "Samurai. Samurai! Not samawry! And he isn't crazy. Don't you know anything about Okinawa and its history!"

"About who?"

"Oh, never mind! Just let him fight with his hands and feet and he'll do just fine."

Maud put her hands on her big buckskin-clad hips and glowered at Candace. "I'd just hoped the poor fella would at least make a good show of it," she growled.

"That's all. But now . . . it'll be pathetic."

The chief grunted and signaled for everyone to get out of the rock ring except Ki and Big Elk. The samurai felt the weak sun on his shoulders. He could smell the pine and hear the breeze rustle through the branches of the forest. He saw an eagle soaring on currents high above the cold valley, and he tasted the smoke and meat from a hundred Crow campfires. He looked at the women and the children and he felt no animosity, not even for the warriors who wanted his scalp.

Big Elk crouched with his knife held out before him, cutting edge turned up. Ki slowly blocked out everything except himself and the huge Crow Indian, who began to move forward. They circled each other, the long, wicked blade of the hunting knife a sinister, gleaming thing between them. Ki's hands were up, his fingers were stiff, the edges of his palms were ready to deliver a stunning if not fatal blow.

The big Indian lunged. He was incredibly fast. Ki jumped back, feeling the blade slice through his *ninja* costume and a thin trickle of blood seep down across his rippling stomach muscles. He had underestimated Big Elk—figured him slow and muscle-bound. He had almost paid for the error with his life.

Big Elk lunged forward again, but Ki was ready. His hand lashed out and struck the Indian on the forearm with such force that the warrior went white in the face as his knife dropped to the ground.

The villagers had been shouting, but now they fell silent. Ki stepped back and then gestured for Big Elk to pick up his knife. The villagers began to babble excitedly. They were shouting encouragement to Big Elk. The warrior roared in fury. Ki knew the big Indian's right arm was broken, and this was proven true when Big Elk grabbed up his knife with his left hand. He was out of patience and came in with a rush. Ki took the Indian's legs out from under him with a sweep-kick.

Even before Big Elk landed, Ki moved in and delivered a knife-hand blow to the giant's neck that left him unconscious.

The entire Crow village stared in disbelief. Buffalo Runner reacted first, ordering two of his men to grab Big Elk and drag him from the fighting ring. The next warrior screamed and charged Ki. The samurai tried another sweep-kick, but the frozen ground betrayed him and he fell hard. The warrior was on top of him in an instant. The Indian was lightning fast, and his knife slashed downward. Ki threw himself sideways and the blade cut through his costume and the muscle of his shoulder. Ki grunted in pain. Then he drove his stiffened fingers upward into the Indian's throat. The warrior choked. He tried to slash Ki's face, but the samurai hit him again and the warrior collapsed, gagging and holding his damaged throat.

"Eeeeii!" a third Crow screamed, bounding across the ring before the samurai could even stand up and meet the charge. Ki dropped and kicked upward. His foot drove into the warrior's crotch like the end of a heavy lodgepole, and the Crow howled in agony and began to roll around, clutching his testicles.

The fourth Crow did not wait his turn. He didn't make the mistake of yelling either, but simply came in low and fast. Ki whirled and decided he had time for only one strike. He chose a *yoko-gerkeagei*, or "sideways snap kick." He raised his striking leg until his knee was in line with his waist. He brought his foot back, cocking his leg until it was next to his knee. When his foot lashed out, its outside edge was angled like a knife blade toward the front of this opponent's knee. When the blow landed, Ki knew that this man would never again attack without being honorable enough to announce a warning. The man screamed in pain as his knee was broken and he threw himself out of the fighting ring.

A fifth Crow came. Ki grabbed his knife-wrist and brought it down across his own knee. The wrist snapped and then Ki chopped him down with a *shuto-uchi* blow.

The sixth Crow did not want to come. Ki saw that and knew that the warrior was afraid but had no alternative but try to save his honor. Ki went at him, and when they closed, he used his knowledge of *atemi* or pressure points to drop the man without serious damage.

There was one warrior left. He carried a lance. Ki smiled. The warrior advanced and feigned a throw twice before he released the steel-lipped lance. Ki waited until the last instant to step aside. Then he grabbed it in midflight.

The Indians blinked with disbelief. They shook their heads as Ki broke the lance over his knee. He grabbed the panicked Crow warrior and slung the poor man out of the ring. Then he picked up the broken lance and walked over to Buffalo Runner and handed it to him.

The Crow chief was in a daze. He had seen seven of his best warriors beaten, and now, as Ki tore open his *ninja* costume to expose his chest, Buffalo Runner understood that *he* was to kill the samurai.

"No," Buffalo Runner said in a hard, guttural voice. "No kill samurai! Samurai Crow warrior!"

Buffalo Runner turned to his people and said something that caused Maud to laugh with delight. "Samurai, you just won your scalp, your wife, and your life as a full member of this village. Congratulations!"

Ki bowed and smiled. Candace began to laugh almost hysterically. A moment later, the Crow Indian began to laugh too.

It was over—until he decided to take Candace and try to make their escape.

★

Chapter 11

Jessica Starbuck had tracked the two Slade men out of the Bighorn Basin clear down into the badlands of eastern Nevada. The Slades had gone straight to Elko, but then their trail seemed to become confused and the pair had begun to travel from town to town. Christmas had found Jessie in a raw little mining metropolis called Pike, and she had telegraphed Circle Star in Texas to tell her people that she hoped to be home before spring.

By now, Jessie knew that the two survivors of the Crow trap were old Napoleon and one of his sons, a vicious killer named Jethro. And by now, Jessie also knew that the pair were ruthless in their quest to track down Buzz Ramsey and young Henry Whitman. She had found the ashes of a hundred of their camps and talked to scores of people who had suffered a painful interrogation at their hands. The Slades questioned anyone and everyone, and if they thought information was being withheld, they were terrible in their punishments. Jessie had found men tortured to death, two small-town lawman gunned down, and women scared almost mindless. But now she had lost even the Slades' trail, and she was discouraged and very worried. There was always the chilling possibility that the Slades had learned of her tracking them and had doubled back around and were now following her in hopes that *she* would find Buzz and Henry.

The weather finally broke and the days grew unnaturally warm for January when she rode into Jumbo. It looked like a dozen other mining towns that Jessie had ridden through—hard, dirty, and filled with miners eager to spend their pay on bad whiskey and worse women.

As always, her first stop was the sheriff's office. Sheriff Clayton Willis sat up quickly when she walked into his small but tidy office.

"Can I help you, ma'am?"

"I'm searching for two men. One's name is Buzz Ramsey, and he has a younger friend, a boy really, named Henry Whitman. Have they been in this town anytime recently?"

Willis cocked his hat back and smiled. He was a small, timid-looking man in his early forties, just starting to go gray at the temples. He looked more like a banker than the kind of man who was supposed to keep a lid on a boomtown. "They were," he said. "Are they friends of yours?"

Jessie weighed her answer carefully. "Acquaintances," she replied.

"Well, if you find them, you can profit handsomely by telling the law," Willis said. He reached into his desk drawer and pulled out a pair of Wanted posters. "As you can see, Ramsey is a worth fifteen hundred dollars now, and the boy is worth five. And that is dead or alive, ma'am."

Jessie read the posters. When she finished, she handed them back and said, "I can't believe that young Henry had anything to do with robbing your bank, Sheriff."

138

"They were in it together and they rode out together. We chased them southeast for thirty miles and finally lost their tracks in a dust storm. Hadn't been for that, they'd both be hung by now." He studied her carefully. "You don't look like the kind of woman who'd get mixed up with Ramsey, though I heard he was quite a ladies' man."

"It's the boy I want. He's no outlaw."

"I'm afraid you're wrong." The sheriff tapped the poster with his finger. "Pretty good drawing of him, wouldn't you say?"

Jessie studied the picture of Henry Whitman once again. In all honesty, she would hardly have recognized Henry. She remembered him as a boy in a stagecoach, a very courteous boy, greatly saddened by the sudden loss of his father. The face on the Wanted poster was that of a man. Henry had grown a mustache, and his plump cheeks had lost their roundness. His face was hard and angular. His eyes seemed dead and his lips were turned at the corners in a slight sneer.

"I can't believe he looks like that," Jessie said, with a shake of her head.

"Well, he does. I saw him and Ramsey when they were in town. Course, that was before the town council decided they needed some law in Jumbo. Before that, rope justice was all they had, and no one had ever robbed the bank before. So in a way, I got Ramsey to thank for my own job."

He peered down at the silver star attached to his vest and rubbed it to a bright shine with the cuff of his sleeve. "Care for a cup of coffee, ma'am?"

"Thank you, I will."

He jumped up and walked over to the door and disappeared for a moment. When he stepped back inside, he said, "There's a fine cafe right next door, and they'll bring over a couple of cups for us."

"Thank you."

"Can I ask you your name and your business in Jumbo, ma'am?"

"My name is Jessica Starbuck and I am helping a friend," Jessie said. "I think that is all you need to know, Sheriff."

A boy brought two cups in to them. When Jessie tipped him a dime he looked as if he had struck it rich. "Thank you, ma'am!"

He raced out. Willis said, "That's my son, Andy. His mother runs our cafe. I got the whole family working."

"What about his education?"

"We don't have a school in Jumbo because there's only about five children in this town. My wife teaches the boy between the breakfast and lunch rush, and then in the mid-afternoon before the supper crowd. As often as not, you can find him and the other ones in here studying all over my office. Sometimes I feel more like a schoolteacher than a sheriff."

Jessie smiled. "He seems like a fine boy."

"He was," the sheriff said, "until you spoiled him with that dime tip. From now on, he'll expect at least a nickel from me. I'd go broke sending out for coffee."

Jessie said, "Do you have any idea where Ramsey went from here?"

"South for a while, then east toward Utah Territory. He's wanted there too, you know."

"So I've been told." Jessie took a sip of coffee. It was good. "Have you seen two big men traveling together? A father and son named Napoleon and Jethro Slade?"

"Name doesn't mean anything to me. What do they look like?"

Jessie shrugged her shoulders. "I've never actually seen either one of them. But I'm told they are both about six-four and mean looking. Thin faces, sharp chins. Both wear beards and mustaches. Napoleon is

140

huge, gray haired, and deadly."

Sheriff Willis shook his head. "It sounds to me like me and Jumbo would be better off if it never sees either of them. But I'll be on the lookout."

Jessie studied him closely. "May I ask you a personal question, Sheriff Willis?"

"Depends on how personal." He forced a laugh. "Try one."

"Have you been a lawman before?"

He blinked with surprise. "Why, no. Why do you ask?"

"Only because the Slades are killers. Jethro has shot two lawmen already, and I'd hate to see that boy of yours lose a father. So if you see or hear of them, get a shotgun and get the drop on them or they'll gun you down. It is possible they may have doubled back on my trail and are letting me take the lead in locating Buzz Ramsey and Henry."

Sheriff Willis wasn't smiling anymore. He looked grim and worried. "Thanks for the advice."

"You're welcome. Is there a decent hotel in Jumbo that I can stay in overnight?"

"Sure. The Mizpah is first rate for this kind of a place. And you already know where to eat."

"And what about a blacksmith and livery stable? The real reason I'm staying the night is that my horse lost a shoe yesterday, and he needs new shoes as well as a good feed and rubdown."

"There's three liveries in Jumbo, but the best one is Jack Adamson's just down the way. You can't miss it."

"Thanks."

Jessie found the livery first and then the Mizpah Hotel, which suited her fine. She asked for a Chinese laundryman and when he arrived, she gave him her soiled riding skirts and blouses. The Chinaman promised to have them cleaned and pressed and at her door by seven o'clock in the morning. Jessie ordered a bathtub to be brought into her room and filled. Then she sat down to write a message to her Circle Star foreman, Ed Wright, telling him about her search and expressing the hope that everything was coming along fine down in Texas. She explained that she wanted to ship two thousand cattle in the spring because prices were going to be very good this year.

"Ma'am? Here's your bathtub, and we'll be bringing up the hot water in just a few minutes."

"Thank you. Close the door behind you, please."

The bellman nodded and exited. A few minutes later, the door opened again and the bellman and his assistant brought steaming buckets of hot water up from the kitchen. It took them five visits to fill the galvanized tub, and when it was done, Jessie posted her letter and tipped them handsomely, asking them to lock her door again.

The bath was a real luxury. Jessie undressed and eased herself in slowly. Her long, slender figure slipped deep into the water, and she sighed with pleasure and leaned her head back and closed her eyes. It was really amazing how a person could forget how much enjoyment and relaxation a simple hot bath could bring. Jessie smiled with contentment and let her cares fall away for a few minutes while she soaked.

She must have dozed off, but she awoke with a gasp and then she choked as a bucket of ice-cold water was poured over her head.

Jessie started to leap out of the tub, but the barrel of a Colt .45 prodded her forehead and Napoleon Slade said, "Come up outta there nice and easy, Miss Jessica Starbuck, so me and Jethro can get an eyeful."

Jessie gripped the metal sides of the tube and listened to the two men laugh at her embarrassment. She realized they must have paid the bellman not to lock the door as he'd exited. "I'm not coming up until you hand me my dress and turn around to face the wall."

Jethro stopped laughing. He was a tall, thin, and wolfish-looking man with a terrible scar down one side of his face. He was scary and his eyes were wild. "You get your ass outta there and onto that bed, woman!" he yelled, starting to unbuckle his pants.

Jessie felt her bones turn to ice. He intended to rape her! "You'll have to kill me before I'll submit to you, Jethro."

He grabbed her long, wet hair and shoved her face underwater and held it there until she thought her lungs would burst. Jessie struggled, knowing she was probably going to be drowned. But suddenly the hand was torn away, and when she raised her head and inhaled breath, she heard the two men arguing.

"She's worth more to us alive than dead!" Napoleon snarled. "She's a rich woman! You want to poke something, find a whore!"

"Ain't no whore I'll ever see has a body like her!" Jethro raged. "Look at that, old man! If it don't make you stiffen up, then you're—"

Jessie heard the sound of flesh striking flesh, and then she saw Jethro lifted off the ground. When he landed on the floor, he was out cold.

Napoleon tossed her a dress, but he didn't turn around. "Put it on and get dressed for a ride," he ordered. "We lost Buzz Ramsey's trail, and I'm sick and tired of waiting for you to find that son of a bitch. Maybe together we can run him to ground."

Jessie dressed quickly, feeling raped by the old man's eyes and hated the way he licked his lips as he watched her. She pulled on her boots and said, "How did you know that I was here?"

"Sheriff Willis and us had a little conference down in his office a while ago."

"*He* told you?" Jessie was disappointed. She'd thought that Willis had more character.

But then Napoleon said, "Willis was pretty stubborn

until we started breaking his fingers one at a time. He'd have yelled real loud except for the gag that Jethro shoved down his throat. I hope he hasn't choked to death yet."

Jessie swallowed. She thought of the boy, Andy. "I'll go with you, but only if I can write a note telling someone to help the sheriff."

Napoleon sneered. "What do you care about him for? He get into your pants or something over that cup of coffee?"

Jessie's cheeks burned. It was clear that this pair of scorpions had been trailing her closely. "The note or no deal," she said.

"Write the son of a bitch," Napoleon growled. "But I'll warn you, Jethro can read some. If you put any extra words in there, he'll have your pretty ass and I'll not stop him a second time."

Jessie wrote the note. Napoleon dipped the same bucket he had used to pour water over her face to pour bath water over Jethro, who awoke, swearing and spluttering. For a couple of minutes, Jessie thought the father and the son were actually going to have a gunfight right in her Mizpah Hotel room, but they got control over themselves and stopped wrangling.

"My horse is at Jack Adamson's livery," she said tersely.

Jethro shook his head. His jaw was already swelling up because of how his father had punched him so hard. It made him look lopsided and even more evil. "Not anymore it ain't. It's with ours in the alley. Come on. Pa says we got us a trackdown to finish up before you and me celebrate."

"The only thing I intend to celebrate," Jessie vowed, "is seeing you and your father dance from the end of a couple of hemp ropes!"

Jethro's black eyes flashed with hatred. "Lady," he

144

said, "taming you is going to be the great pleasure of my life."

He shoved her out the door, and they slipped out through the rear of the hotel and mounted their waiting horses.

Jessie did manage to drop the note off to help Sheriff Willis in the hallway. As she was led away, she just hoped the man would be saved before he choked to death.

"We're going to find and kill Ramsey if we have to search for a hundred years."

Jessie climbed on Sun and patted his neck apologetically. "Sorry you didn't get the rest and rubdown I promised."

"Hell," Jethro spat, "that ain't nothing but a long-legged horse."

Jessie studied the horses that the Slades were riding. Her heart sank when she noted that they were also exceptional animals. Had they been on ordinary cow ponies, she'd simply have waited her turn and then broken free and outrun them. Maybe Sun could beat these Slade horses, but it seemed clear that they would make it a close race. Close enough for them to yank their guns and shoot Sun right out from underneath her.

They galloped out of Jumbo, and when they reached the edge of town, Napoleon reined his horse in and said, "Here's the deal. You help us find Buzz Ramsey, and we spare the boy."

"Is that the same deal you made his mother?" Jessie asked coldly.

Jethro's voice shook with pent-up fury. "You either make the deal or I throw you down in the dirt and take you right here and now. Which is it?"

Jessie took a deep breath. She had managed to slip a derringer into her boot-top, and when the moment came that Jethro so eagerly anticipated, she would kill him.

Then, because her derringer carried only one shot, she would probably be killed by old Napoleon. But in the meantime, she knew she needed to stay alive. The only good thing about any of this was that if the Slades were with her, at least she knew that Buzz and Henry were still alive.

"I asked you a question!" Jethro shouted.

"It's a deal. My help for the boy's life," Jessie said meekly.

Jethro smiled. "See, Pa? I told you she was going to settle down and mind me once she realized I meant business."

But Napoleon wasn't quite so sure. "Woman," he said, squinting his eyes, "I don't trust you even a tiny bit. You're fixin' to fix us good, but it ain't going to happen."

Jessie raised her head. It would not do well to act too submissive. "I thought we just made a deal."

"That's right, we did, for a fact. Now, which way do you reckon they rode outta this town the day that Ramsey robbed the Bank of Nevada?"

Jessie remembered Sheriff Willis telling her that he and a posse had chased Buzz and Henry southeast for thirty miles.

"Don't lie to us," Napoleon warned, "or I'll let Jethro have you right now and kill the boy later."

"Southeast," Jessie confessed.

"See, Pa? That's what the sheriff finally said after I broke his third finger."

"So you knew all the while."

"Yeah," Napoleon said. "I figured we'd test you just to make sure you abide by your part of the deal and tell the truth. It's a damn good thing you did."

Jessie shivered as they reined southeast. Napoleon Slade had just given her an indication of how devious and clever he could really be. Now Jessie began to understand that she had better not make the mistake of underestimating the man's intelligence and cunning.

★

Chapter 12

Buzz Ramsey left Henry in their creekside camp and rode out long before dawn. He cut across the sagebrush-covered hills and climbed to the head of a long grade, where he studied the old stageline road. He tied his horse in the rocks and yanked his Winchester free from his saddle boot. As daylight broke to the east, the sun was coming up as bright and shiny as a new penny, and the heat of it felt good on the wide rack of his shoulders. Buzz moved down from the rocks to a good vantage point beside the road. He peered out across the immense vista of southeastern Utah and saw the Mormon town of Hooker, Utah.

He rolled a smoke and inhaled deeply. The sharp tang of the tobacco in his notsrils helped to pull him awake and at the same time calm his jangled nerves. Things had not gone very well since leaving Jumbo. The damn posse had chased them so far into the desert that he and Henry had lost their horses to thirst before they had been able to return to another settlement. And then in the next decent-sized mining town, Buzz had lost his money in a forty-eight-hour card game, and had been forced to kill the man who'd marked the deck. But once he had finished the shooting, it turned out that the cards hadn't been marked at all!

He and Henry had barely escaped with their lives. The two horses they'd grabbed to get out of town had been damn near worthless, and if it had not been for a passing freighter, who let them hide under his tarp, they'd have been caught and hung for certain. In exchange for his silence, the freighter had gotten every last cent they owned.

So now here he was, broke again, and with half of the lawmen in Utah after his hide. It was enough to make a man wonder what had gone wrong with his life. Why couldn't he have just settled down and married Candace Whitman and turned over a new leaf? She'd owned a house and she had some money.

I should have married the woman, he thought miserably. But then, the goddamn Slades had come to town and that had been the end of it.

Buzz smoked his cigarette down and then rolled another. He noticed that his hands were a little shaky, and that worried him. If things went according to plan, not a shot would be fired, but he needed to be steady just in case. He did not intend to kill anyone else, but that was *their* choice. Life had kicked him around pretty hard, and Henry was fed up with running from the law—not that he blamed the kid.

Maybe the Mormons have a strongbox full of gold, he thought. *Maybe this is finally the "big one" I have been waiting for all my life.*

He saw the stagecoach roll out of Hooker, and he checked his pocket watch. It was exactly 6:45 in the morning, and the stage was right on time. There was a gold and silver mine in that town, and everyone said that they sent the ore out on Wednesday morning. The stagecoach was on its way to Salt Lake City to replenish Brigham Young's coffers. Buzz had also been told that it only had one shotgun guard, because only fools dared to rob Mormons in their own territory.

Buzz hoped it had only one guard. If the box was filled with gold and money, he had a plan. He was going to travel south, down to Texas, and find himself a small ranch, a place where he could run a few head of horses as well as cows. The new ranch house would have to have a nice porch for Candace and himself to sit under during the heat of summer afternoons.

As he watched the stagecoach leave a rooster-tail of road dust out of Hooker, Buzz tried to think of how all the good things in life would come to him after this last job. This was no life for him, or for Henry. *At least*, he thought, *I never let Henry break the law.*

The stagecoach had to slow down for the grade, which was exactly as Buzz had planned. He wiped his hands on his grimy pants and levered a shell into his rifle. There was just a driver and one shotgun guard. Probably a couple of passengers inside, half asleep and unwilling to buy into any kind of trouble.

The team of stage horses was straining in their traces. Buzz could hear the crack of the driver's whip as they labored up through the rocks. He lost sight of them as they navigated the curves, only to find them again when they came back around.

Buzz pulled a bandanna up to hide his face and stepped out from the rocks and into the road. "Hold it!" he yelled.

The driver hauled in on the reins, but the stupid shotgun guard acted like he had been robbed before. With amazing quickness, he drew down his weapon. Buzz shot him through the shoulder. The man screamed and was knocked off the coachbox, to land in the dirt. He was hit bad and thrashing in agony.

"Anybody inside get out right now!" Buzz shouted, moving around so that he could peek into the coach and cover the passengers. But there was just one older couple and a man who looked like he might be a banker.

Buzz motioned to the woman. "Lady, if you know any doctorin', then you had better take a look at the guard before he bleeds to death."

The woman, a large and stern-looking sort, hurried around the coach to help the guard.

"Goddamn you," the banker-sort hissed. "You'll swing for this!"

"Shut up and throw your wallet and watch into the dirt. You too, mister," he said, gesturing to the old man. "Also any jewelry you're wearing."

The banker pulled off a diamond ring that looked to be worth a couple of hundred dollars. But the old married guy refused to hand over his jewelry.

"All I have is my wedding ring, and you're not taking it!"

"What about your watch and your wallet?"

The man reluctantly pitched them at Buzz's feet.

Buzz let the man keep his wedding ring. He had never robbed citizens except from across the surface of a poker table, and it left a bad taste in his mouth to do so now.

"How is he?" Buzz shouted to the woman.

"I think he's dying." The woman said it almost matter-of-factly, and it made the hairs on Buzz's neck raise. He thought the woman must have seen a lot of dying to sound so collected. "He can't be. I aimed for the upper part of his shoulder!"

"Well, you shot low! I think he's taken a bullet through the lung."

Buzz swallowed noisily and shook his head. "That just can't be," he whispered. In his whole messed-up life, Buzz had prided himself that he had never killed a good man for doing his job. On the contrary, he had rid the frontier of a lot of bad ones. "Driver, pitch the strongbox over the side. You other two men get over there and put the guard back into the coach and head on back to Hooker and find a doctor!"

The driver didn't move, and Buzz was so upset about maybe killing the shotgun that he almost forgot the strongbox. When the guard was loaded inside and the passengers were all in their seats, he said, "Where's the strongbox?"

"Ain't none today." The driver smiled wickedly. "Try us next week. You might have even worse luck if I got anything to do with it."

Buzz almost went crazy. He threw himself up on the coach and nearly shoved the driver off his perch. In a near rage, he discovered that the driver was telling the truth. There was no strongbox.

Suddenly, the driver took a swing at him. Buzz saw it coming and reared back. He lost his balance and dropped nearly eight feet to the ground. The wind was knocked out of his lungs and he was stunned for an instant. The man who looked like a banker found a gun inside the coach, and poked it through the window. He took aim and fired.

The bullet caught Buzz in the upper leg, and he grunted with pain. The man fired again and missed. Buzz raised his gun and put a bullet right through the man's forehead.

Now the woman screamed and lost her composure. The driver lashed his team and, as Buzz lay in the dirt, the coach rolled away. Not fast, because the grade was steep for another twenty yards and it was all the team could do to gain some momentum, but by the time they disappeared over the crest a few seconds later they were moving fast enough to outdistance a man with a bullet in his thigh.

Buzz told himself not to panic. He tore off his cloth vest and ripped it into strips, using his hands and teeth. He fashioned a tourniquet and tied it a couple of inches above the leaking wound. Almost at once, the heavy flow of blood slowed. Buzz took a deep breath. He crawled over and picked up the wallets, ring, and both men's pocket watches. The wallet held only eight dollars. That was another disappointment, because the man he'd killed had the look of success about him, and such men usually carried big money.

Buzz used his rifle to push himself to his feet.

He groaned and felt dizzy. He began to hobble toward the edge of the road. Suddenly, he heard a thundering of hooves and looked up to see the stagecoach come flying over the crest of the hill, bearing down on him. Buzz tried to throw himself out of its path. He didn't quite make it.

The right swing horse hit him. He felt himself being lifted from the road as if snatched up by a mighty hand. Then he was thrown twenty feet, struck a rock, and went crashing over the side of the hill. He blacked out.

When he awoke, the sun was still rising, and he found himself fifty yards below the crown of the road, in a bad fix. His leg had stopped bleeding, but it had stiffened up. When he hopped up on one foot, he found that he was weak and very unsteady.

But all of that was instantly forgotten when he shielded his eyes from the bright ball of sun and saw that the stagecoach had already reached Hooker. And even as he watched, he saw a posse come storming out of town. Buzz knew they were coming after him.

"Oh, sweet Jesus!" he groaned as he whirled around and attacked the steep mountainside. He fell and clawed his way back up to the stagecoach road. The wound began to throb mightily and, when he looked down at it, he saw that it had reopened. Fresh blood was filling his pantleg.

Buzz turned to look at the posse and cold sweat burst from every pore on his body. They were closing very fast. Only a few miles out now. He had to get to his horse and get out of this country!

It seemed to take him forever to reach the animal. When he did, the damned thing spooked at the smell of

Buzz's blood. Buzz swore viciously, but finally he managed to climb into the saddle though the effort drained the last of his strength.

"Ya!" he cried, spurring the horse out of the rocks and up the stage road towards his camp. He had to warn Henry, and then they would escape. It would be especially tough this time, but the alternative was a hangman's noose. He had killed one stagecoach passenger for sure, and maybe the shotgun guard as well. But he had not wanted or intended to harm either.

With one hand on the saddlehorn and the other holding the reins, he used the horse under him hard. The pain in his leg was so overpowering he could not think straight any longer. All he knew was that his only chance was Henry. Henry was smart, and he had been through this enough to know how to get them out of this fix.

Two miles away, Henry doused his fire and broke camp because he knew he might have to ride out fast. He saddled his horse and even tightened his cinch. Though Buzz had promised there would be no more bank or stagecoach robberies, when Henry had awakened at dawn and found his partner gone, he had anticipated the worst. Buzz had lied to him again and gone off somewhere to rob someone or something.

Henry had decided right then that it was time their trails forked. He wanted no part of being an outlaw. He was a man now, man enough to understand that Buzz was on a one-way path to the gallows or a posse's bullet.

The thing of it was, Buzz had saved Henry's life, and his mother's too. Henry figured that meant he owed Buzz Ramsey his loyalty. But exactly how much was the real question. Henry decided it stopped short of owing the man his company on the gallows.

No, sir! When Buzz returned, he was going to split the blankets and head on back to Texas. He'd find his mother and figure out a better way of making a living than being the partner of an outlaw. He just had the feeling that things were going from bad to worse with Buzz. No longer did he believe the man's stories about how he was going to settle down with his mother on some little cattle ranch and find happiness and tranquility.

The sound of racing hoofbeats made him spring to his feet. He saw Buzz come flying down the road, and it was clear that the man was shot. He was barely hanging onto his saddle, and was in real danger of falling.

Henry vaulted onto his own horse and raced forward to meet and help him. He felt a deep dread building in his chest, and when he saw the amount of blood that Buzz had lost, his worst fears were confirmed.

"They're after me hard," Buzz gasped. "Can't be more than a mile or two."

"You can't go much farther!" Henry cried.

Buzz sat up straight. His face was etched with pain and there was no color in his face at all. He reached out and grabbed Henry so hard it hurt.

"Goddamnit!" he swore. "I'll hang if they catch me! I need your help. Don't let me down now, for Chrissakes!"

"All right," Henry said. "But this is the last time I'll try to help."

"Fine! Now tie me into the saddle and take my reins and let's go!"

Henry did as he was ordered. But he was in such a state of agitation and time was so short that he didn't do a proper job of tying Buzz into the saddle. Henry could see the dust of the posse just over the hill, and so they ran with the sound of gunshots ringing in their ears.

Henry knew they had no chance of escape in open country. A long chase would kill Buzz for certain. The man would simply bleed to death. So Henry decided the only thing that he could do was strike out through the brush and rocks and hope that he could somehow find a place to hide.

It was wild country, rocky and hard to negotiate. Big clumps of brush, dry washes filled with smooth rocks, hidden arroyos, and painted canyons that might or might not lead to freedom.

Henry was riding for their lives. He kept looking back, and whenever he did, he saw the posse. It was closing the distance.

They were flying up a brush-choked wash when a big covey of quail exploded out from under them. Henry's mount shied, but he managed to grab leather and stay seated. Buzz wasn't so fortunate. His horse began to buck as the quail scattered across the wash and then disappeared into the brush. Buzz, though tied in, slumped and fell, dangling alongside the shoulder of his plunging horse. The blood and the unnatural position of the man made the spooked horse go crazy. Henry tried to hang onto its reins, but they were jerked from his hands.

Buzz cried out weakly. His head was now all the way down to cinch level and Henry knew that the man was going to get tangled up and maybe stomped to death in the next few moments.

Forgetting the posse, he drew his pocketknife and rode in close. He slashed the ropes that bound his friend to the crazed animal and grabbed Buzz by the collar and dragged his head up and then pulled him off the bucking horse.

"Freeze!" a man with a star on his chest yelled. "Hands up!"

Henry did not let go of his friend. He managed to get his own horse under control, and, when it slid to a standstill, he hopped off and eased Buzz down onto the rocky wash.

"I said get your damn hands up!" the sheriff yelled again as his posse crowded around them, guns drawn and aimed.

Henry took a deep breath and raised his hands. In a second, the sheriff was flying off his horse and yanking his gun from his holster.

"I got Wanted posters on both of you. Hooker is mighty proud to be the ones that will see you hang."

Henry shook his head. "I've never broken the law!"

"That's right," Buzz said in a faint voice. "He's innocent as a babe."

"The hell he is," the sheriff growled, grabbing Henry and yanking him to his feet. "One of you men tie this young bastard up with his hands behind his back and his feet bound together under his horse's belly."

A big man asked the question that they all wanted answered. "What about this pair of murderin' sons of bitches? I say we find the nearest tree and hang 'em outright!"

"They both go to jail to await the judge."

"Circuit judge won't be through Hooker for three whole weeks!"

The sheriff said, "That can't be helped. This isn't a lynch mob, boys. We operate by the law of the territory, and Judge Storm will sure as blazes make the waiting worthwhile on both counts."

Buzz opened his eyes. "I never meant to kill that passenger. I killed him in self-defense."

"Self-defense!" The sheriff's blue eyes grew flint-hard. "You killed the mayor of Hooker, and its leading citizen. Deacon Potts was about the most respected man in this county. A lot of folks are sure going to enjoy seeing you swing."

"What about the shotgun guard?"

"Dead too." The sheriff grabbed Buzz by the shirt-front. "I just wish we could hang you twice, you bastard!"

156

They yanked Buzz to his feet and tied him back onto his horse. Henry was so scared he was sick to his stomach. The posse figured to hang them both, even though he had been nowhere close when Buzz had killed the two men earlier that morning.

Henry gripped the saddlehorn with both hands and stared at the ropes tied around his wrists. He was too young to die for crimes he'd never committed. He had not yet even had a woman, though he'd been close a time or two. He hadn't seen an ocean or ridden a train. Hell, there was so much he had not done yet!

"I want to live," he whispered to himself.

"What'd you say?" the sheriff demanded.

Henry looked up and was ashamed because his eyes were stinging with hot tears and because he was afraid of dying. "I said I wanted to live."

"Too bad, son. You should have thought of that before you tied in with a thievin' killer like Buzz Ramsey."

Henry looked away quickly. The sheriff was right, but also wrong. There was a lot of good in Buzz. He'd saved his mother, and he was not a cold-blooded killer like some he had killed. Nope, he just wasn't. Trouble was, sometimes Buzz just stepped across the line, and then he got into bad fixes. But he wasn't mean, and he wasn't a bloodthirsty killer.

Three weeks until the circuit judge came through. He'd still be sixteen in three weeks, but out here in Utah Territory, they'd hang a five-year-old if they caught him stealing licorice candy.

★

Chapter 13

Jessie rode feeling battered, dirty, and exhausted from too many hours in the saddle and not enough sleep. But deep inside her, there burned an invincible fire that no amount of abuse could extinguish. Jethro had not tried to attack her, but that was only because there had been no opportunity for him from atop a horse. And during the few hours that they had stopped to rest the horses, they had dropped from their saddles, too weary to feed themselves.

But the chase was almost over. They had learned that Buzz Ramsey and Henry were jailed in Hooker, Utah Territory. They were both alive and about to swing from a rope for the murder of a stagecoach guard and a passenger.

When Napoleon and Jethro had learned of this news they had initially been furious, for it robbed them of the chance to kill Buzz slowly. But as they galloped toward Hooker, both father and son had adjusted their thinking, due in no small part to a chilling idea that old Napoleon had conjured up.

"What I'm going to do," he stated, "is convince the hangman that he ought to tie a strangling noose so that they choke to death real slow."

Jessie had been horrified as the two men laughed obscenely.

"You ever see a man choke to death at the end of a noose, Miss Starbuck?" Jethro asked, winking at his father.

Jessie shook her head. She had never even seen a hanging, and she had no plans for watching one in Hooker.

"Well," Jethro said, delighted at the chance to explain things to her in great detail. "If the hangman does his job right, the neck is broken just as neat as you please. Course, the hung man still flops around a little, but they tell me he is already dead and the jerky stuff is no more than reflexes that won't quit. Sorta like when you wring the neck of a chicken."

"Shut up," Jessie said as they galloped side by side.

Jethro pretended not to hear her. He continued. "But a man who strangles—"

Jessie swung her whip in a backhanded motion, laying a red welt on Jethro's cheek. The man howled and reined his horse toward her but Jessie dug in her spurs and let Sun have his head. The stallion had been waiting for his chance and, though they were riding in rugged country, he shot out ahead of the Slades as if he were a pronghorned antelope. He bounded over brush and rocks, and Jessie lay flat in the saddle as she pulled first a horse-length and then more ahead of the two heavier men.

"Don't shoot that horse by accident!" Napoleon shouted. "It's worth plenty."

"Come on!" Jessie urged as a bullet whistled past her ear. "Run!"

Sun was in better shape than the Slade horses, and Jessie was a superior rider. She'd noticed that over the past week, and now she used this important advantage as she spotted a wide gully off to her right. She aimed Sun directly for it as bullets winged past her like a swarm of angry yellowjackets. She felt one pluck at her sleeve, and then she felt Sun gather himself underneath her and spring out across the wide gully.

Sun felt to Jessie like he hung suspended in mid-air for almost a full heartbeat. The gully was six feet deep and fifteen feet wide. When they struck the far side, Sun's hind legs dropped, and he clawed madly to pull himself upright.

A bullet cut Jessie across the shoulder, but then her horse scrambled up and ran like the wind.

Jessie twisted around in her saddle. She saw the Slades through a cloud of dust and a hail of bullets. Jethro had tried the same leap, but his horse had failed to clear the chasm. He was down in the gully, hatless. The pair was both shooting to kill now, but the distance between them and Jessie was widening with each passing second.

Jessie stayed flat and let the wind blow hard in her face. All the weariness and depression lifted from her as if by magic. She was free again, and less than forty miles away lay Hooker. If Henry Whitman were proven guilty of murder as she had been told, then Jessie could do nothing to save him. But if he were guilty simply by his association with Buzz Ramsey, then that was another matter entirely.

She was still thinking that way when she galloped into the Mormon community of Hooker and dismounted in front of the sheriff's office.

The office was closed. Jessie turned around and headed for a gunsmith's shop, and when she entered she got right down to the purpose of her visit. "This derringer is the finest model that has ever been made. I bought it from the factory, and you can see that the mother-of-pearl handles are inlaid with gold."

The gunsmith was a studious-looking young man who wore wire-rimmed spectacles. He took the offered weapon and examined it almost lovingly before he said,

"I never saw a prettier one in my life, miss."

"Do you think it is worth a hundred dollars?"

"Oh, my yes! But if you want to sell it, I'm afraid I don't have a hundred dollars. I'm sorry. I know I will never see a finer derringer."

Jessie knew she needed a few dollars to send a telegram and feed and house herself until Ed Wright wired her funds. "I'll take twenty dollars and a serviceable Colt .45 in trade," she said.

The gunsmith blinked. "I'm afraid that I would be cheating you, miss."

"Then cheat me," Jessie said hurriedly, knowing that the Slades were no more than two or three miles behind her. "Throw in a holster and a box of bullets if it eases your conscience. But I need them quickly."

The gunsmith smiled. "Very well." He reached into his glass case and pulled out a nice weapon and began to tell her all about it. Jessie cut him off with a word. "Thanks."

She strapped on the holster and made sure the gun was loaded. When she stepped out onto the street, she was ready and more than willing to face the two men who had held her captive.

Jessie hurried over to Sun and untied him from the hitching rail. She took him around behind the sheriff's office and tied him to a tree. Then she rushed back to the main street and planted herself beside the sheriff's office to wait for whoever arrived first, the sheriff or the Slades.

Sheriff Frank Potter arrived first. Jessie hurried inside and closed the door shut behind her.

"Jessie!" the two prisoners cried almost in one voice the moment they recognized her.

Jessie walked back to their cell. She studied their smiling but wan faces. She would not have recognized Buzz Ramsey. He looked to have aged twenty years. There were dark circles under his eyes and he wore a thick bandage around one thigh. Henry didn't look a good deal better. He was very thin, and even taller than she'd remembered. Someday, if he lived, he would be a big man. "You've really gotten yourselves into it this time, haven't you?" Jessie whispered to them.

Henry opened his mouth to defend himself but no words came out. He turned away, and Buzz said, "I deserve to hang, but not Henry. He never broke any laws, and he was miles away from the holdup. I'm going to swear to that in court tomorrow."

Jessie's heart sank. "The trial starts tomorrow?" She had been hoping to have enough time to send for one of the Starbuck lawyers. That hope was now dashed.

"Yeah." Buzz touched her cheek through the bars. "How's Henry's mother?"

Jessie didn't want to tell him that the poor woman had been kidnapped, just as she herself had. And there was no certainty that Ki had been successful in freeing her from the Crow Indians. So, because she did not have the heart to load any more grief on this pair, she just said, "Fine."

Henry brightened a little at the news. "Miss Starbuck," he said, "I got to ask you a favor. If I swing, and it looks like I will, given the way the people here are talking, then I want you to promise not to tell my mother. She begged me not to leave, but I did anyway. Will you do that?"

"Can you swear to me you have never robbed or murdered?"

"I can, Miss Starbuck. I'll swear it in court, and I'll swear it before you right now."

"And I'll swear he's innocent too," Buzz Ramsey said.

Jessie nodded. She curbed her tongue, knowing it would do no good to scold Buzz for allowing the young man to ride the outlaw trail with him this past year. So instead she just said, "I'll be in court tomorrow to help you. I've had some experience in legal matters."

The sheriff had been listening and now he chimed in to say, "Miss Starbuck, it don't matter how rich you are. Those two are going to hang. I got Wanted posters on them both, and Judge Storm is a hanging judge."

Jessie turned to face the man. "Henry Whitman says he's innocent of murder or robbery, and I believe him. A man is supposed to be innocent until proven guilty."

"What's to prove? He and Ramsey are partners. He was waiting for Ramsey and trying to help him escape with whatever loot they could steal from this community. And even though he didn't pull the trigger, he tried to save the man that did."

"So give him a jail sentence!" Jessie shouted. "Not a hangman's noose!"

Potter turned away from her. "It isn't my duty to make the laws or to pronounce judgment. Talk to Judge Storm tomorrow in court."

Jessie heard the drumming of hoofbeats outside. She hurried to the window and looked out into the street to see Jethro and Napoleon gallop past.

"I want you to arrest *them*," she said. "For murder and kidnapping."

"You got any proof?" Potter asked, gazing at the two dangerous-looking men who had just ridden into his town.

"Just my word."

"Not good enough."

Jessie held her anger in and told Sheriff Potter how the Slades had killed several men in Nevada and had promised to see Buzz Ramsey strangled to death in the hangman's noose.

Sheriff Potter was not impressed. "I have no reason to arrest the Slades. No proof of lawbreaking within my jurisdiction. And the fact that they have promised to see Buzz Ramsey strangle at the end of a rope is, frankly, very appealing to me and the citizens of Hooker."

164

"I'm telling you that they have killed men on the trail we followed!"

Potter flushed wish anger. "And I'm telling you that I have received no Wanted posters on anyone named Slade. Furthermore, what they did in Nevada, Colorado, Wyoming, or any other state or territory is not my concern. What I am concerned about is seeing that these two murderers hang by the neck until dead!"

"If they see me in here, they may want to make sure *you* are dead, Sheriff."

The lawman's eyes widened. He was middle-aged, and no hero. "I got nothing to do with them or you," he said nervously. "And as long as they break no laws, they'll see justice carried out."

"Justice?" Jessie shook her head. "I have a bad feeling inside that, in Henry Whitman's case, this town doesn't know the meaning of the word."

The sheriff walked back to his desk. "Excuse me," he said, "but I have work to do."

Jessie opened the door. The Slades were there, staring at her hard. "Sheriff, you've got more work on your hands than you even suspect."

With that, she closed the door and walked to her horse. She mounted up and rode back a block to a boarding house that advertised rooms for rent. Jessie dismounted, tied her horse up, and went inside. She might be wrong, but she figured that as long as Napoleon and Jethro figured that it was dead certain Buzz was going to swing, they would behave themselves.

It just figured that they wanted to see the condemned man strangled to death.

The trial began in the town's makeshift courtroom, which also doubled as the town meeting hall. It was packed an hour before Buzz and Henry were led in under heavy guard, and Jessie had to stand up against the side wall. It was just as well. Napoleon and Jethro

165

swaggered in, ripped two of Hooker's citizens out of their chairs, and seated themselves in the last row. Jessie would not have dared to turn her back on that pair, even in a crowded room.

The sheriff and the bailiff led Buzz Ramsey and Henry to their benches. They wore shackles on their ankles and manacles on their wrists. Jessie heard the angry hissing sounds of the people, and knew that they would accept no other verdict than a death sentence.

"Hear ye! Hear ye!" the bailiff intoned. "The Territorial Court of Utah is now in session. The Honorable Clayton T. Storm presiding. God Bless Brigham Young and the President of the United States of America!"

Judge Storm slammed his gavel down hard and plunged the courtroom into instant silence. "This court is now in session. Bailiff, you may read the charges."

The bailiff read the charges very quickly. In the case of Buzz Ramsey, it was two counts of murder in the first degree, in addition to horse theft, stagecoach robberies, and the robbery of the Bank of Nevada in the town of Jumbo.

Jessie sighed. Buzz was lost. She knew that he deserved the gallows, but she could not help but feel badly for the man. Maybe that was strange, but it was the way she felt.

The bailiff continued. "In the case against Henry Whitman, we have accessory to murder and robbery charges both in Utah and Nevada Territories. He is also a horse thief; the horses on which they were apprehended being stolen from Nevada. They are both branded with the Circle Bar brand of a Mr. Amos B. Sutton, who has sent a sworn affidavit of his ownership, duly notarized for this court's consideration."

Jessie's heart almost broke. Horse thieving alone was usually a hanging offense.

But Buzz Ramsey jumped off his wooden bench and shouted, "*I* stole *both* them horses! He was sleeping when I did it, just the same way he was when I left to rob your damned stage!"

The judge slammed down his gavel. "Order in this court! Order! Bailiff, if the prisoner speaks once more from the floor, I order you to gag him!"

Buzz was yanked back down to his bench, and the trial began—only it wasn't really a trial. There was no defense, just a reiteration of the charges. Sheriff Potter was asked to read the Wanted posters twice, word for word. Other men got up and testified about how they had seen the stage come barreling into Hooker and found two dead men on it. Others testified that they had joined the posse, and then had overtaken Buzz and Henry up in the mountains.

It was late afternoon when the prosecution finished up. The people were getting restless. "Buzz Ramsey," the judge said, "do you have anything to say in your own behalf before I pronounce your sentence?"

Buzz stood up shakily. He gazed across the room at Jessie and winked. Then he turned back to face Judge Storm and said, "All I have to say is that I wished I hadn't been forced to kill those two men. I am damned sorry about that. I'm also sorry that there was no gold or silver in the strongbox, because it means I'm going to swing for risking my life for nothing. But I'm tired of living, so the hell with it. Bad luck has dogged me for years and I'm going to cheat any more of it coming my way."

Buzz took a deep breath and continued, his voice steady and strong. "I got only two things to be proud of in this life, and one is to say that I have killed a lot of bad men that needed hanging worse than I do now. I probably saved a few lawmen's lives, and I am proud that I never back-shot anyone— though, like most professional gamblers, I have always been a double-dealin' cardsharp. The other thing I am proud of is that I never let this boy here do a single damned unlawful thing—

not that he would have anyway. He is guilty of nothing but being fool enough to stick with me because I helped his ma once. I taught him how to use a gun and how to play poker. I guess I did a mighty poor job of teaching him how to live upright and honest like the rest of you in this room."

Buzz looked down at his manacles, then up at the bench. "I ask you, Judge Storm, not to be hard on this boy. He is innocent and he deserves to be free. I'm . . . I guess I'm begging you, Judge."

The courtroom fell into a deep silence which was broken only when the judge finally cleared his throat and said, "Buzz Ramsey, I pronounce you guilty as charged and sentence you to be hanged tomorrow at noon."

He turned to Henry and frowned. "How old are you, boy?"

"Sixteen."

"Do you have anything to say in your own defense?"

"No, sir. Only that I am not guilty of anything unlawful. My ma taught me the Good Book, and I know I should have tried harder to stop Buzz. In that, I failed. But that's all. And if I hang, it will be with a clear conscience."

The judge took a deep breath. "This court is recessed for the sentencing of Henry Whitman until tomorrow morning at nine. Court adjourned."

The courtroom burst into excited whispers. Jessie felt limp. And she had no idea what tomorrow's verdict would be.

Chapter 14

Ki lay beside Candace, listening to the storm beating at the walls of their tipi. Their small fire flickered and made dancing figures that fed Ki's rich imagination. It was just after midnight, and the samurai knew that the snow was falling hard and that he was ready to escape with Candace. In truth, their weeks together had been idyllic, and if it had not been for worrying about Jessica Starbuck, he might have been content to linger in the Crow village. But the thought of Jessica facing the Slades was always in his mind. It was time to go, and yet, as he lay beside the woman under his buffalo robes, he felt a deep reluctance. He had come to care deeply for the Crow people, who treated him as a warrior.

He had learned more from these Indians, and now he understood why Maud Slade had decided to cast her lot with them. The Indians had many positive qualities, and a philosophy of life that was much closer to the samurai's than that of most white people. They did not, for instance, strongly attach importance to ownership. They shared with each other, and though they would fight to the death to protect their own hunting grounds, they did not believe that the earth could be claimed by anyone. It belonged to all, like the sun, the moon, and the stars.

Ki also admired their ability to be like children. It was not unusual to see men playing with their babies and their sons. Men did not do that in Japan, and not much on the American frontier, either.

Ki arose and dressed quickly. He stepped outside and studied the camp and felt the cold kiss of snow. The snow was wet, and stuck to his face and clothing. But wet or not, it was falling heavily and would quickly obliterate the tracks of their horses. For this reason, it was important to use this opportunity while it lasted.

Ki went back inside and awakened Candace.

"Is it time?"

He nodded. "Dress warmly. We have a long ride ahead of us."

"I'm prepared and more than ready," she said, casting aside her robe and dressing in the semi-darkness.

Ki nodded. They had been waiting for just such a late winter storm to hide their departure. Their small cache of food and supplies was packed in deerskin bags.

"I wish I could say goodbye to Maud," Candace said with regret.

"She'll remember what the Indians would say in explanation."

Candace turned around and stared up at him. She smiled with amusement. "And that is?"

"When a white man is saddened to say goodbye, he feels it in his head and his tongue speaks. When an Indian is saddened to say goodbye, he feels it in his heart, and the heart has no tongue."

Candace kissed his cheek. "I think that if you could remain among the Crow without worrying about your samurai pledge to Jessica Starbuck, you would gladly do so. You have also taught these people much about *te* and your *bojutsu* skills."

"I taught some of the younger ones," he admitted.

"Those who would really listen and use those few samurai skills with wisdom."

"Do you think that these people would try and stop us from leaving?"

"I would have to kill Big Elk to take you away from this Crow village. And if I did that, then Chief Buffalo Runner might be forced to have me killed in return. Why risk such unpleasantness?"

"Yes," Candace said, picking up her deerskin bags to indicate she was ready to leave. "Why, indeed?"

They caught up their ponies and used the rope and horsehair bridles of the Crow. They had no saddles and would ride bareback, a fact which worried Candace, since she was not an accomplished horsewoman.

With the wind at their backs, they rode silently out of the village, the hooves of their ponies making soft, swishing sounds against the snow. When Ki turned to look back, there was just enough light to see that their tracks would be filled over by daybreak. With luck, the snow would keep falling all morning and their departure might not be noted until late afternoon.

By then, Big Elk would have gone hunting and, upon his return, perhaps realize that it would be foolish to search for Candace.

They stopped at the base of a rocky mountainside just after daybreak, less than a hundred feet from the rushing Bighorn River. Ki found driftwood under a huge boulder and got a fire going. They had nothing to cook with, but they did roast some smoked elk meat and warmed their hands and feet.

Candace was so cold that the chattering of her teeth was even louder than the river. When Ki reached out and touched her forehead, his suspicions were confirmed. "You've got a fever. Why didn't you say something?"

"I'll be all right."

"I think we had better build a shelter and wait out the last part of this storm," the samurai said.

But Candace wanted to keep going and put as much distance between them and the Crow Indians as possible. "I can go on," she said stubbornly.

"No," the samurai said. "It would be a mistake. Down here in this canyon, we are at least out of the wind. Maybe you will be able to travel later in the day."

Candace did not argue. She nursed the fire while Ki collected driftwood and branches to use as a shelter. They piled them around the base of a boulder and encompassed their small fire. The day stayed cold, but their boulder reflected the fire's heat back to them, and they were very comfortable.

"Ki?"

He had been sitting cross-legged before the fire, his thoughts on Jessica and the Slades. Now he raised his head to look at her. "Yes."

"I've never dared to ask you this before, but . . . but are you in love with her?"

"Of course."

"That's what I thought," Candace said miserably.

"No it's not," the samurai replied. "Not quite, anyway. You see, I love Jessica like a sister."

"You mean you've never—"

"No."

"But you have wanted to."

The samurai shrugged his shoulders. "She is a beautiful woman and I am a man."

Candace nodded. "Of course. I didn't mean to pry. I just thought that, if we get out of this country alive and back to Texas . . ."

She let the sentence trail away like the smoke from their campfire. Ki fed the fire. "What did you think?"

"If Jessie can get Henry away from Buzz Ramsey, I'd like to move closer to your Circle Star ranch."

172

Ki smiled. "Jessie still wants you and Henry to come and live on Circle Star."

"I might do that. My mother is dead and my house in Alder, Texas, was burned to the ground. But what I really wanted to know was if you and I could still ... you know."

"Of course I know." Ki gathered the woman in his arms and held her tight under the buffalo robes. His fingers caressed her most sensitive bud of pleasure. "I'd take you right now if you weren't in the grips of a fever."

She bit his neck and shoved her hand into his pants and squeezed his manhood into an erection. "I've got a fever for *you*, Ki. One that only you can quench."

Ki smiled and buried his face in her hair. He let her guide his turgid rod into her hot wetness.

And with the storm blowing snow, they settled into the rhythm of lovemaking that they had learned in a Crow tipi. As Candace squirmed with pleasure and grasped his powerful buttocks with mounting desire, Ki kissed her forehead and noted that she already seemed cooler. Maybe they would wait out this snowstorm under this rock, making love.

Three hours later Ki's horse lifted its head suddenly and whinnied. Ki pulled up his pants and buttoned his shirt, then reached over and threw dirt to kill their small campfire.

"What is it?" Candace whispered.

"I don't know." The samurai crouched and moved forward, out from the shelter of the rock. "It could be Big Elk and the Crow. It could be a wild animal."

Suddenly he heard a sound above and to his right. Ki started to spin on the balls of his feet, but an Indian struck him a glancing blow across the head and he crashed to the earth, rolling, feeling blood wash down his right cheek. Candace screamed. Then an arrow cut through the falling snow. As Ki jumped up and faced the Indian who had struck him with his war axe, he realized that he was fighting a Cheyenne, the enemy of the Crow.

The warrior rushed him, and Ki fell back as if in fright. When the Indian swung his axe, Ki timed his sweep-lotus perfectly and caught the Indian under the chin. The man went down, choking.

Ki grabbed the fallen war axe, knowing that his *shuriken* blades were unsuitable in the wind and the blowing snow. The axe spun from his hand and its blade drove into the bowman up on the rock.

Ki heard a distant call and realized that the pair he had killed had been the advance scouts of a war party. They must have blundered upon their two Crow Indian ponies and assumed they would catch a pair of enemy hunters.

But now, the rest of the Cheyenne were coming to investigate. Again, Ki heard the high, shrill call of the Cheyenne. And though the samurai did not understand its exact meaning, he felt sure it demanded a reply.

Ki cupped his hands to his mouth and imitated the call as best he could. The wind beat at the noise and whipped it into the mountain, but for a moment he must have satisfied the rest of the Cheyenne.

"Let's get out of here while we still have a chance," he said.

Candace needed no urging.

They gathered their robes and belongings and ran through the snow to their horses. Ki helped Candace mount; then he swung onto his own horse. They drove their heels in, and the horses began to buck through the knee-high snowdrifts and climb up from the river through the trees.

But the Cheyenne were expecting this. They cut off the only escape route, and the air was filled with their cries for blood and scalps.

"Come on!" Ki yelled, turning his pony around and heading back toward the river with the Cheyenne in full pursuit. Back down the mountainside they plowed. Their horses were blowing dragon-clouds of steam. When they reached the Bighorn River, Ki raced his horse into the water and yelled, "It's our only chance!"

Candace's mount hesitated at the edge of the icy river, but with the Cheyenne charging their own painted ponies down the mountainside, Candace's horse jumped and began to swim. Ki guided his horse toward a small, snow-covered island about twenty yards from shore. The river was too treacherous to cross to the far side. They would drown, and if they were even thrown into the water, they would freeze in minutes.

"Look!" Candace shouted. "It's Buffalo Runner and Big Elk!"

Ki swung his horse around and saw that she was right. The Crow had followed them and now, seeing their enemies had invaded their land, they were furiously attacking the Cheyenne war party.

The samurai got his horse swimming back toward their camp, and when its hooves struck solid ground, he let out a wild Crow yell and charged the Cheyenne.

The battle was over in minutes. As the Crow chased the few surviving Cheyenne eastward, Ki and Candace faced Chief Buffalo Runner and Big Elk.

"You are better at their language than I am," Ki said. "Tell them it was good that we fought this last time together."

Candace did as Ki asked. When she was finished, Ki added, "Tell them we must go back to our own people but will miss the Crow and will always remember them well." He was watching Big Elk. The huge warrior's face was expressionless and hard. It would not have surprised the samurai if Big Elk had drawn his knife and hurled it straight for the heart.

But when Candace translated Ki's message in sign

and spoken Crow language, it was Big Elk who nodded first and then raised his hand in the sign of peace . . . and farewell.

"Let's get out of here before he changes his mind and decides he can't bear to let me go," Candace said.

"Good idea."

They rode back up the mountainside, through the battleground and the bodies of the dead Cheyenne. They rode over the mountain and then angled their horses so that the snow-covered Bighorns were to their right. They were heading southeast to Cheyenne to check and see if Jessie and Henry were there. And if not, then they would keep riding all the way to the Circle Star ranch in Texas.

★

Chapter 15

Judge Storm banged his gavel down hard. "This court is now in session! Will the defendant, Mr. Henry T. Whitman, please rise and stand before me for sentencing."

Jessie took a deep breath and exhaled slowly. She hardly knew young Henry, but she did not believe he was an outlaw, or even a horse thief. She believed Buzz Ramsey when he said Henry had never broken a single law.

The real question about to be answered, though, was whether or not the Mormon judge believed in Henry's innocence as well.

Henry, shackled, was led to stand before the judge, who cleared his throat and addressed the courtroom. The judge said, "Rarely have I erred in favor of a defendant. It has been my experience that most men are guilty as sin of many crimes, very few of which they are held accountable for. I am known as a hanging judge, and that title does not slander or even displease me. I am a hard man, but the law is clear and equally hard on the lawless. Outlaws, thieves, rapists, murderers—I have seen and hung them all. But now I am torn between my heart and my mind."

The judge leaned forward. "My mind tells me to hang young Whitman. He did, after all, ride with a murdering thief on a long outlaw trail. Surely he must have known that it would bring him misfortune, even death. And so, I cannot believe he is completely innocent. And yet, I spoke to him last night in the privacy of the jail cell, and during our long, long discussions, I became convinced that the young man was sincere in his quest to save Buzz Ramsey from the kind of sad end he faces in just a few hours. Henry Whitman's crime was his innocence of heart and his foolish belief that he could save a lost soul. In short, his heart was in the right place, even though his head was not."

The judge straightened. "I have been accused of being a hanging judge, but I am also a merciful judge. And because of Henry's youth and sincerity, I have decided to pardon him completely..."

The courtroom exploded with shouts and controversy. Some men were furious; others were just as convinced that the judge had done the right thing. Jessie closed her eyes and let tears of relief slide down her cheeks. "Thank you, God," she whispered. "And thank you, Judge!"

"Silence in my courtroom!" Judge Storm shouted, banging his gavel down hard. "Silence!"

The courtroom quieted and the judge continued. "I have decided to pardon him with the condition that he leave Utah Territory and never again cross our borders. This is my decision. This court is adjourned."

Henry turned, and his face was also awash with tears of joy. He held out his wrists and the bailiff unlocked his manacles and then his shackles. Jessie pushed through the throng to Henry's side and hugged him tightly.

"How would you like to be a cowboy on the biggest, finest ranch in the state of Texas?"

"Yeah," he whispered. "I sure would like that."

"Good. Let's get our horses and get out of here right now. If Ki has been successful, we'll find your mother either in Cheyenne or at Circle Star."

"I can't leave Hooker just yet," Henry said quietly.

"But why not?"

"I want to be with Buzz until he . . . he hangs today at noon. I want to walk right up to the gallows, just in case he needs a friend."

Jessie nodded. "I understand. I wholeheartedly approve. I'm sure that would mean everything to Buzz."

She turned around to leave, and that was when she noted that the Slades were glaring at Henry. A chill passed through her as she read their murderous intentions. Never mind that that boy had not killed any of their kin. Somehow, they equated Henry and Buzz Ramsey, the cause of all their misfortunes. Henry and Buzz were partners; therefore, they both deserved to die.

Jessie was glad she was wearing a gun again. Judge Storm may have just granted Henry Whitman his life, but the Slades figured they were the last word.

The Slades turned and stomped out of the courtroom. They would probably head for the saloon, get liquored up, and then go to enjoy the hanging. But after Buzz Ramsey hung, Jessie knew that that pair of Wyoming killers were going after Henry.

Jessie shook her head. She did not want to go to the hanging, and yet . . . yet she dared not leave Henry unprotected from old Napoleon and Jethro Slade once Buzz was dead—not even in the center of a hundred spectators about to watch Buzz Ramsey swing into eternity.

"I'll have horses saddled and ready to ride the minute it's over," she told Henry.

"I'd like that fine," he said. "I'll never look back again without remembering Buzz."

They walked outside. Henry fell in beside the sheriff

on his way to the jail where he'd join Buzz for this last hour of his wasted life. Jessie headed for the livery to have Sun saddled and to see if she could trade her fine-tooled saddle for a fast horse for Henry. Never mind that they would be riding bareback. Once they reached Cheyenne, she would have money wired up from Circle Star, enough to get them back to Texas in style.

By eleven-thirty, almost the entire town had gathered at the south end of Hooker, where the gallows stood with a fresh rope thrown over its beam and its trapdoor hinges glistening with new lubricating oil.

The mortician served as the hangman, and he was dressed all in black with a top hat and tails, starched white collar, and a jovial manner that nauseated Jessie.

"Here he comes!" some of the kids shouted, running ahead of Buzz and the grim-faced Sheriff Potter.

Jessie looked at Buzz closely. If the man was afraid, he did not show it by his expression. No, she had to admire the way that Buzz marched ahead, manacles dragging in the dirt, but head held high and eyes locked on the gallows that awaited to take his life.

Her eyes turned to see Henry. He looked distraught. To see the pair, you would have thought it was Henry instead of Buzz who was about to hang.

Jessie stepped into their path. "Goodbye," she said. "I'm sorry it had to come to this end."

"Nobody's fault but my own," Buzz said, keeping his voice steady. "My last wish is to kiss one more beautiful woman." He struggled to add, "Would you . . . could . . ."

Jessie put her arms around his neck and kissed him full on the mouth. She was surprised to feel again the hot sting of tears in her eyes. Somehow, Buzz Ramsey swinging from a rope was all wrong.

Buzz swallowed with an effort. "Thanks," he said. "Are they here watching?"

180

"Who?"

"The Slades."

"Yes. In the front row. I think they will try to kill Henry. So I'm getting him out of here before they realize we are even gone.

"They'll still just hunt you down too. He'll never be free of them as long as they are alive."

Sheriff Potter shoved Buzz forward. "Come on. Let's get this over with, Ramsey!"

"Goodbye," Jessie said, taking Henry's arm and stopping him at the gallows stairs, which led up to the terrible trapdoor.

Henry was trembling. On the verge of getting sick.

Jessie felt little better. She said, "Let's go now. The horses are right over there. Bareback riding is not my favorite, but I was almost broke. There is nothing more you can do for Buzz. I'm sure he'd rather not have you watch."

Henry didn't even seem to hear her. But he nodded and allowed himself to be turned away from the gallows.

Suddenly, Jessie heard a man shout. She looked up on the gallows and saw Buzz grab Sheriff Potter and spin him around and grab his sixgun.

A woman screamed and the crowd scattered in panic. Potter was knocked flying as Buzz raised the sixgun in his manacled fists and shot Jethro Slade between the eyes. But amazingly, Buzz held up his next shot for the fraction of a second it took for old Napoleon to draw his weapon and pull the trigger.

Buzz staggered with a bullet in the chest. Then he seemed to regain his balance. He looked right down into Henry's eyes and winked.

"You killed my last boy!" Napoleon screamed. He raised his gun to fire again. Buzz expended his final ounce of life and shot Napoleon Slade through the brain.

Jessie and Henry rode out of Hooker, Utah. Neither of them would ever look back. They had no need to. The last of the Slades was dead, just like Buzz Ramsey had planned.

Watch for

LONE STAR AND THE LOST GOLD MINE

sixty-eighth novel in the exciting
LONE STAR
series from Jove

coming in April!

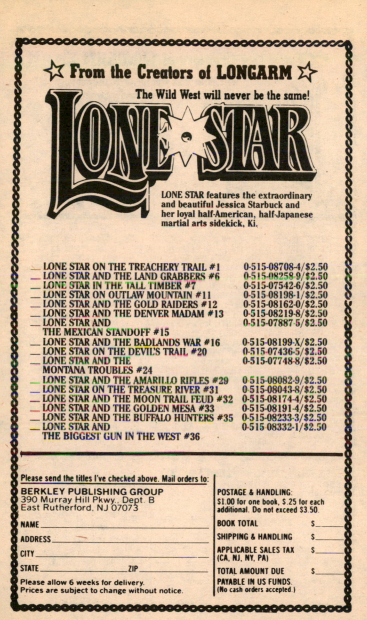